COMMUNITY LIBRARY

FORT LOUDOUN

REGIONAL LIBRARY SERVICE

LOOK, read, enjoy and
treat me just fine

REMEMBER to return me when
it is time

SO I CAN keep busy everyday
Bringing joy to others
along the way.

THIS is the kindly thing to do
A nice way to say

THANK YOU!

TWILIGHT AT MONTICELLO

WILLIAM PEDEN

Twilight at Monticello

HOUGHTON MIFFLIN COMPANY BOSTON

1973

First Printing c

Copyright © 1973 by William Peden.
All rights reserved. No part of this work may
be reproduced or transmitted in any form by any
means, electronic or mechanical, including photo-
copying and recording, or by any information storage
or retrieval system, without permission in writing
from the publisher.
ISBN: 0-395-15462-6
Library of Congress Catalog Card Number: 72-9020
Printed in the United States of America

FOR PETCH

I am closing the last scene of my life by fashioning and fostering an establishment for the instruction of those who come after us. I hope that its influence on their virtue, freedom, fame, and happiness will be salutary and permanent. An inscription on the base of a statue of The Founder, The Grounds (West Lawn), the University of Virginia, from a letter of Thomas Jefferson to John Adams

AUTHOR'S NOTE

THE CHARACTER of John Rodney is to a degree based on my affectionate recollections of the late John Dos Passos. All the other characters and events of this novel are fictional, and any resemblance to actual people and events is purely coincidental.

Over the years I have been indebted to the work, in print and in progress, of many Jefferson scholars, particularly to my dear friend, the late Adrienne Koch Kegan, professor of history, the University of Maryland; Dumas Malone, biographer in residence, the University of Virginia; and James A. Bear, curator, the Thomas Jefferson Memorial Foundation. George Garrett, professor of English, the University of South Carolina, and Paul Murray Kendall, professor of English, the University of Kansas, have read the manuscript and given me much valuable assistance. Mrs. Smith Mayo, of Princess Anne, Maryland, first used the title of the novel some thirty years ago, in an article in the *Virginia Quarterly Review*.

Parts of this novel were written while I was visiting professor at the University of Maryland, and I am grateful to that institution for much released time. And to my colleagues at the University of Missouri, especially Noble Cunningham, I owe thanks for many things.

CONTENTS

CHAPTER 1

UP, UP, AND AWAY!

Yet I will not believe our labors are lost. I shall not die without a hope that light and liberty are on steady advance. Thomas Jefferson to John Adams, September 12, 1821

As THE PLANE bumped along the runway Margaret caught a quick glimpse of the Library of Congress through the hazy rectangular window, and Raymond closed his eyes and reached for her hand as he always did before takeoff. Raymond had not liked the looks of the plane before they boarded it at the Washington airport. It looks, he had said only half jokingly, as though it should have been grounded with the Eisenhower Administration; let's rent a car and drive instead. But she had pooh-poohed the idea: we've checked our bags through, she said, there's nothing wrong with the plane, and besides Craig has probably planned to meet us at the airport in Charlottesville. So they had boarded the plane, as she had known all along that they would, Raymond grumbling good-naturedly and fidgeting while they waited on the runway for clearance. Now at last, after a takeoff that left Raymond looking slightly nauseated, they were airborne, rising slowly above the green-gray curve of the Tidal Basin and flying upriver to avoid the restricted White House zone, past the surprisingly white needle of the Monument and the long rectangle of the Kennedy Memorial Center, the blur of Georgetown University and the District suburbs. Beyond the Chain Bridge the plane leveled off and turned inland toward Virginia and Raymond opened his eyes cautiously; beneath them the development houses looked like spilled white beads on a dun-colored carpet.

"I feel better," he said, as much to himself as to Margaret. He smiled, loosened his seat belt, and removed his dark glasses, polishing them and examining them critically before returning them to the pocket of his jacket. He was breathing easily now; he was happy, she knew, to be off the runway, and on the way to Charlottesville.

"It's good to be on our way," he said. "We'll be there before you know it. It's a very short flight."

Margaret Green turned down a page corner and closed her paperback copy of *Under the Volcano*; unlike Raymond she always read during takeoffs and landings. You will ruin your eyes, he always insisted; you should take better care of them; if your eyes were as bad as mine you would take better care of them.

"I can hardly wait. I've heard so much about it, about everything. All those friends of yours, and Monticello and the banquet and everything."

Raymond smiled and straightened out his legs and absent-mindedly fingered the flattened bridge of his nose.

"It'll be quite a rally, I expect, never a dull moment."

"And I'm so anxious to see Craig again. I wonder . . ."

She paused as Raymond placed his fingers on the back of her hand and gently nudged her elbow, at the same time glancing forward where a dark little man with an enormous halo of black hair was examining the magazine rack. He wore a wide-lapeled double-breasted knitted purple suit; white cuffs protruded inches from his many-buttoned sleeves and an incredibly wide pale green tie spilled over the confines of his soft white collar.

"Look," Raymond whispered. "Up there, by the magazine rack. Do you know who that is?"

Margaret rubbed her forehead. "The little man? No, but he looks familiar. Wasn't he . . . wasn't he at the airport?"

"That's right. He's Fogel Freiberg."

"Who?"

Raymond started to groan softly but halted abruptly as the little man, as though aware of their presence, swung his dark eyes in their direction; beneath curling black hair and a narrow forehead his heavy eyebrows formed an almost unbroken *T* with his hawkish nose. Raymond smiled hesitantly and leaned forward as though about to nod, but after a flicker of semirecognition the black eyes dismissed him and returned to the magazine rack. After examining several of the folders with obvious irritation, the little man finally removed one from the rack — *Current History*, Margaret noted, as he lurched toward them to half tumble into his seat beside a woman with a pale and beautiful face.

Below them, the land was opening into a gently rising patchwork of field and pasture still more oat colored than green from the long winter except for occasional swathes of reddish earth dotted at intervals with a lone farmer on a tractor.

"It's good to see that again." Raymond took a deep breath and smiled. "I bet the air's better there than in Missouri."

"You don't really love Virginia, do you? You're not *really* glad to be going back to Charlottesville, are you?"

"You know I am. I really am. It's hard to believe I haven't been back in . . . three, can it be three years . . . ? Some time before we were married, anyhow." Again he stroked the bridge of his nose and gazed toward the magazine rack. "I wonder what that joker is up to. He can't be going to Charlottesville. Not for Founder's Day. Or could he? And in that Buster Brown outfit. That would sure go over big at Monticello!"

"But he's not one of the Jefferson people, is he?"

"Fogel Freiberg? Lord, no." Raymond's voice was contemptuous.

"Well, who is he then?"

"He's a poet. At least he *was* a poet. But . . ."

"Oh, *that* Freiberg. Of course. *Fogel* Freiberg. How stupid of me. He's a good poet, Ray." Margaret leaned forward as though to study the occupants of the seat ahead of them. "They were at the airport in Washington, I remember now, of course . . . He was with that incredible woman. The Eurasian-looking one. With the spaniel. She's beautiful. The woman, that is. And her clothes! That's why I didn't think much about *him*. I was looking at her. Stunning. And so expensive."

Again Raymond smiled. "You *would* remember her clothes."

"Any woman would, Ray. And I've seen her before, somewhere. Or pictures of her. She's a model, maybe. Or an actress. I can't remember which, but I know I've seen her before. And she's Freiberg's wife. At least she's wearing a wedding ring."

Raymond regarded her with bemused wonderment. "You don't recognize Fogel Freiberg. And in that suit." Without thinking, he leaned forward, craning his neck until Margaret cautioned him with a restraining hand. "But that Asiatic Madame Bovary up there, you notice she's wearing a ring . . . I wonder." He ran his fingers gently over his nose. "By golly, Meg, I bet they *are* going to Charlottesville!"

"But you said he's not one of the Jefferson people."

"That's right, he isn't. But it could be because of *Native Roots.*"

"Of course. *Native Roots.* I should have remembered . . . Do you know him? You started to speak to him at the airport. I didn't know you knew him."

"I've met him." Raymond's response was dour. "He gave a poetry reading at Virginia once when I was an undergraduate. He'd gone there, you know. Only one year, I think, or maybe it was only a semester; anyhow, he left sometime during his first year. He couldn't stand the place; he was always bitching about something. Always bitching, always yakking, that's what I heard."

"People didn't like him very much?"

"You can say that again. But after he'd won the Pulitzer Prize I guess the English Department felt they had to invite him to give a reading. Even after that poem attacking the University." Raymond paused reflectively and rubbed his jaw. "I didn't like him when he gave that reading, and I don't like him now."

"Oh Ray, that's silly. He's a good poet, really. He hasn't written much lately, at least I haven't seen any of it, but he's a good poet. Why don't you like him?"

"Look, I hardly know the guy, I just heard him give a poetry reading, twenty years ago it must have been. I never knew him at Charlottesville. We didn't, uh, run in the same circles, you might say. But I did see him later, a couple of times, much later. When I was doing research on my dissertation at the Library of Congress."

"Oh? When he was poetry consultant?"

"I guess so, something of the sort. I was just about finishing my dissertation. He didn't remember me but I told him I'd heard his, uh, reading, and we had a cup of coffee together. I told him about the work I was doing and later, it was some time after *Native Roots* had started, I sent him an article. He didn't take it. He turned it down."

"Oh? That's too bad. What was it about?"

"Sally Hemings. It was published later, in one of the quarterlies, the *Virginia Magazine of History and Biography*. Before we were married."

"Who's Sally Hemings? The name rings a bell but . . ."

"Sally Hemings was one of the slaves at Monticello. Monticello Sally, Black Sally, sometimes she's known as."

The buzzer sounded forward, the FASTEN YOUR SEAT BELT sign flashed on above them, and then the static-fragmented voice of a stewardess was announcing that they would soon be approaching the Charlottesville airport.

"I'll tell you more about her later; I thought we'd talked about this before. It's a very big issue now."

From the corner of her eye she watched Raymond fumbling with his seat belt; invariably, it seemed, whether in a car or plane, he had difficulty with seat belts. Sometime, he often said, if he ever wrote a book that made any money, though the Lord knows academic historians don't usually make much money from their books, he would buy every known type of seat belt and install a merry-go-round horse in his study and spend hours until he had mastered the mysteries of seat belts. Shortly after their marriage, driving home from her parents' in Ohio, they had seen a beautiful prancing merry-go-round horse in a small-town antique shop and both of them had admired it greatly, had even started to buy it, but finally, reluctantly, had decided they couldn't afford it. When my next novel is published, she had said, we *will* come back here and we'll buy that horse . . .

"Will you help me with this thing?" He turned in mild irritation to Margaret. "I've nicked my thumb."

She clicked the belt buckle into position, and he smiled and glanced quickly over her shoulder as the plane began its descent: could that sudden flash of blue-green be the roof of the Rotunda? No, the approach to the airport was from the other side of the University Grounds. He put on his dark glasses and reached for Margaret's hand; a man's a fool, he sometimes said, ever to set foot in an airplane, and he closed his eyes until the plane bumped to a landing. Only then did Raymond breathe his customary sigh of relief; he was, she knew, mentally checking his belongings: wallet, tickets, and baggage checks; change for porter, topcoat in the rack above, portable typewriter beneath the seat. The familiar routine completed, he turned to Margaret.

"Have everything? Let's not forget anything."

She nodded and smiled.

"Let's not hurry," he said as the plane taxied slowly to the terminal. "Let's wait till most of the others are out. We'll have to wait for our luggage anyhow. I think they're always pretty slow with the luggage here."

"Do you think Craig will meet us?" Margaret peered through the window. "I don't see him."

"Maybe. I imagine so. No real need to, though; he's probably out of his mind with all the details. He knows we know our way around here."

"What about the Freibergs?"

"I still can't believe that joker's been invited here for Founder's Day . . ."

She silenced him with a warning squeeze on the arm, and he sat quietly as the plane approached the ramp and jolted to a stop. Headed by Fogel Freiberg and the dark-haired woman, shapely even beneath her tailored mink-trimmed wrap, the passengers clogged the narrow aisle. Raymond, she knew, was feeling disorganized and slightly weak in the knees, and lightheaded, as he usually was after even a short flight: if I ever have to consult a psychiatrist, he often said half-jokingly, the first thing I will have to tell him will be how much I hate planes. Why are you so uneasy when you're in a plane? the psychiatrist would ask. I don't know, he would reply. It's nothing to worry about, really, the doctor would continue, many people feel this way. But did you, perhaps, have any bad military experience involving planes? No, he would reply, I don't believe I was ever in a military aircraft. I was commissioned immediately after graduation and — She nudged him and with some difficulty he retrieved the typewriter from beneath his seat and rose unsteadily from his chair.

"Are you sure you have everything?" he asked again, and as she nodded he led their way up the rapidly emptying cabin, hesitating at the top of the landing platform to focus his eyes against the still-bright afternoon sun. Would Craig be there, she wondered, remembering simultaneously that Raymond had said he did not have the slightest idea where they would be staying. Then, with a sudden flow of pleasure, she saw the mountainous figure of the curator at the gate to the terminal: good and thoughtful Craig, with a million and one details to take care of, how characteristic of him to meet them at the airport. Enthusiastically Raymond started to return Craig's wave, but was halted in the act, topcoat in one hand and typewriter in the other.

"Be careful," he said over his shoulder to Margaret, nodded a thank-you to the stewardess, and made his way gingerly down the slightly swaying steps and to the terminal gate.

"Ray, and Meg! How good to see you."

Craig Babcock's greeting was as warm as the April sun, his soft Tidewater voice pleasantly incongruous in so enormous a man. He kissed Margaret's cheek with courtly delight and embraced Raymond, whose still-shaky legs trembled beneath the onslaught.

"By Cock, it's good to see you both. I've a thousand things to tell you all. How was your flight?" He squinted at Raymond. "You look as though you could use a drink, *viejo*. Still hate flying as much as ever, I'll bet." He swung his massive curly head toward Margaret. "You're looking wonderful, Meg. It's been too long since we've seen each other. How's the new book going? And yours, Ray?"

Without waiting for answers he squired them toward
the terminal building, still talking constantly.

"Armistead and Helen got in from Cambridge yesterday." Craig's amiable face reddened slightly. "I'm worried about Armistead, Ray; I must talk with you about
this tomorrow. Webster knows about the Chair. It hasn't
been announced officially, but he's known for some time.
Armistead's accepted it, of course, I was sure he would, but
it won't be made public till tomorrow night, at the lecture. *And Carla.*" Craig closed his eyes and shook his head
slowly. "You know how *she's* reacting to all this. . . .
Problems, problems. But the weatherman's on our side
— good weather, warm and sunny. Matter of fact, it never
has rained on Founder's Day, not in the last few years anyhow. But it snowed once. Can you imagine, Meg? Snow
on the fruit trees at Monticello for Jefferson's Birthday!"

Raymond threw up his hands in simulated alarm. "Slow
down! You haven't changed a bit. You never would let
me get a word in edgewise!"

Craig slapped him on the shoulder, and again Raymond's knees buckled.

"Nonsense, *viejo.*" He turned to Margaret. "Ray's
always been the big talker, you know. But let me get
your bags. You all wait here, I'll be right back."

The curator shouldered his way into the terminal, and
returned shortly, followed by a porter pushing their bags
on a handcart. As they made their way toward the parking lot, he stopped suddenly and groaned.

"Good Heavens! The Freibergs. I've forgotten the
Freibergs!"

CHAPTER 2

SIESTA AT THE
BOAR'S HEAD INN

Love me much, and love me always.
Thomas Jefferson to Maria Cosway,
July 27, 1788

M ARGARET, naked beneath the king-sized towel with its crest of a grinning boar's head, stretched her legs luxuriously and smiled as she listened to Raymond's off-key singing in the bathroom.

What is Vir-gin-ee-uh?
Who are the Cav-a-leers?
Those who walk along the Lawn
When the eve-ning sun is gone
And Vir-gin-yuh's moon ap-pears?
This is Vir-gin-ee-uh
. . .

Raymond's singing and the hissing of water stopped simultaneously; she envisioned him stepping gingerly from the shower, the dark pelt on his chest sleekly wet, his strong arms and shoulders in marked contrast to the beginnings of his professorial stomach. It is good to be here: *Charlottesville and Thomas Jefferson Monticello and the University but what a beginning Craig will have his hands full before all this is over how silly and wonderful the drive from the airport that April-green rolling country Ray's right Virginia is the most beautiful state Craig so flustered and the Freibergs so silly at almost having been left at the airport . . .*

"And have you all met the Greens, Margaret and Raymond Green?" Craig had asked after he had retrieved the Freibergs from the terminal.

Freiberg, dark hair writhing like a Medusa's, had paused, momentarily ignoring Raymond's outstretched hand before unenthusiastically extending his own while Raymond's "Yes, when I was at the University" hovered uneasily in the air above them. And to make matters worse, Craig had led them to his station wagon unaware that they had brought their dog with them. Only then, as he was offering her his arm, had Mauve Freiberg broken her self-imposed silence.

"Mess-taire Bab-cock, you 'ave forgot-tain our dog!" For the remainder of the drive Fogel Freiberg had stared gloomily out of the window while Mauve remained silent, her incredible breasts rising and falling like tethered falcons beneath her parted mink-trimmed wrap, her almost-Oriental violet eyes studiously avoiding the other occupants of the station wagon. Even their first sight of the University Grounds — tennis courts, red-brick white-columned buildings, an ascending series of grassy slopes, trees of varied shades and tones of new green bathed in the unbelievable apricot glow of the early afternoon sun — had failed to evoke any response from the Freibergs until suddenly their champagne-colored puppy had raised its head, uttered a dismal howl, and thrown up on the floor of the station wagon.

At the recollection of Craig Babcock's consternation and the ensuing embarrassed confusion, Margaret laughed aloud. In the bathroom the buzzing of Raymond's electric razor immediately stopped.

"What in the world are you snorting about?"

"Just the Freibergs, darling. You were so good not to show that you were irritated. And then that poor dog!"

Raymond's *humph* was noncommittal. "Meg."

"Yes."

"My razor *does* work better here than in Missouri. I told you it would. The air *is* better here. The razor doesn't drag as much here as it does at our prairie home."

Margaret suppressed a smile. "Of course, dear."

The buzzing recommenced. How that man hates to shave. And he had looked so splendid with his beard: shortly after their marriage she had persuaded him to try a Vandyke and a small mustache, but after a few days he had abandoned the project. The buzzing again stopped and she smiled as he noisily blew the shavings from the razor.

"Don't hurry, darling — too much, that is — but aren't we supposed to meet the Freibergs and . . . Who else did Craig say? Dorsey Jack Somebody and someone named Tolliver, I think? In the lounge here?"

"That's right. I'll be through in a minute. We've got lots of time, though; let's have a drink."

"I could really use one."

She left the bed, the towel dropping from her body. For a long moment she studied her reflection in the mirror above the Sheraton dresser. Not too good, she thought, running her fingers lightly over her small, high breasts: I can't compete with la belle Freiberg there. But not too bad, either, even if my legs are a bit on the skinny side — though Raymond, bless him, says they're just right. Her face, she knew, though neither spectacular nor indeed even memorable, had good lines and good bone structure, with its straight nose and her clear gray eyes and a forehead topped by thick waves of auburn hair. A good Middle Western small-town face. And her hips and belly were above average, at once both well-fleshed and firm, and highlighted with what Raymond admiringly had labeled the last of the truly great Renaissance navels.

"Stop admiring yourself, Mrs. Green." He was standing behind her, smiling bemusedly. "You know, you're a very attractive woman." His eyes traveled across her body. "And I love that outfit."

Instinctively she had bent over to retrieve the towel but after a moment of hesitation tossed it aside with the toe of her foot, straightened up, and faced him.

"Oh, Ray, do you think so?"

"You know I do."

She hastened to him and put her arms around his waist.

"I'm glad. So very glad. I don't know how I got along before we met. Forgive the bromide, darling, but it seems as though I've known you, loved you, all my life. How *did* I get along without you?"

Raymond flushed, shifted from foot to foot, then grinned. "Just lucky, I guess. By Heaven, madam, you are beautiful." He leaned over and brushed her breasts with his lips.

"Ummmmmm, that's nice, Professor Green." She tightened her fingers against his shoulders. "Ummm, good heavens, *very* nice indeed." She glanced through half-closed eyes at the great bed. "That's delicious, Ray, but . . . stop just a minute, darling, don't you think . . . I mean, we don't have much time, do we . . . they'll be waiting for us before we know it, won't they?"

Reluctantly Raymond took a backward step, hesitated, and again looked at her intently as she leaned over and retrieved the towel, wrapping it loosely around her waist. "I, uh, guess you're . . . oh, to hell with them," he said, reaching for the towel. "This is a holiday, we've got lots of time."

"Are you sure? I mean I'd love to, but wouldn't you be so tired?"

"I won't be tired."

"Stop talking then," she said, coming to him swiftly, "and do that again, what you were doing. Oh Lord that's delicious . . ."

. . .

"I can really use that drink now," she said later as she lay and watched her husband carefully pouring the golden bourbon from the leather-covered flask she had given him on his last birthday. "You know, I'm really very nervous about meeting all your friends; after all, Craig's the only one I know and I haven't seen him since he stayed with us after those meetings in Missouri."

"There's nothing to be nervous about. The 'Mafia,' well, they're just like anybody else. There's nothing for you to be nervous about."

"Oh, but there is. I wish I'd had time to read more about Jefferson. I still know practically nothing about him, except for your book, and the Mafia, they're all experts, and old friends of yours and everything."

She paused, and gratefully took the glass from Raymond, shaking her head and waving her free hand helplessly around the room with its hand-hewn pine beams, dormer windows, and paneled bed alcove — they got *that* idea from Jefferson, Raymond had told her after the liveried bellboy had bowed himself out of their room. "And I'm not accustomed to motel rooms with fieldstone fireplaces; honestly, Ray, I'm nervous."

They touched glasses and he sat down beside her on the massive bed. "I'm not accustomed to this sort of thing either, as you, uh, know; it's really pretty pretentious. And that receptionist, you know the pale titless creature in the granny outfit — I guess she's one of the new breed coeds; they didn't have many coeds at the University when I was a student — I thought she was pretty uppity. Someone ought to break it off in that little bitch. But don't let it worry you." He raised his glass. "And as far as the *experts* are concerned, you'll like them. The Mafia . . . they're odd, but you'll, uh, like them. Most of them, anyhow."

"Oh, I hope you're right. But who's Thorpe Tolliver? I haven't heard that name before, have I?"

"Don't believe so. He's a librarian. I didn't know he was going to be here. He's with the Library of Congress. The manuscript division. Thorpe Tolliva', spelled T-a-l-i-a-f-e-r-r-o. I know him, or rather I knew him, pretty well. We went to the same high school in Maryland and were in graduate school here at the same time for a couple of years — he did his dissertation on Patrick Henry — and then we taught a while together, at Woodberry Forest, but I haven't seen him recently. He's been at the

Library of Congress quite a while, almost as long as I've
been at Missouri. He works with the Jefferson manuscripts; he does annotated bibliographies, checklists, that
sort of thing. I'm surprised he's going to be here. He's
O.K., I guess, but, well, Thorpe's really pretty much of a
jerk."

"And Dorsey Jack. Is he a jerk, too?"

Raymond stirred his feet slightly.

"Dorsey Jack's a she, darling."

A swift flicker fluttered along Margaret's spine and she
took a long sip and studied her husband before replying.

"Oh? I'm . . . I'm glad there're going to be some
other women around. Dorsey Jack . . . did you say Morgan? . . . I hope she's not going to be like Mauve Freiberg."

"Don't worry about that, honey. Dorsey's good-natured,
she's no Mauve Freiberg. She's with the Institute of Early
American History and Culture. At Williamsburg. Dorsey's an archivist."

Margaret felt a momentary surge of relief. An archivist
with the Institute of Early American History and Culture.
At Williamsburg. *A fat little thing, probably, with sensi-*
ble shoes and snub-nosed pencil stuck in the bun of her
hair probably drinks too much half-emptied pints of
vodka stashed away behind the folios . . .

"What else does she do? Other than being an archivist?
I mean, what's she doing here, for the Founder's Day program? Is *she* that good?"

Again Raymond paused, a bit too long, she thought.

"Well, Dorsey's no great scholar, that's for sure, but
she's, uh, competent. Very competent. And she gets

around." Again Margaret's spine tingled. "And she's done one good book, small in a way, but not bad, not at all bad."

"Oh, what?"

"It's a book on Maria Cosway."

"Maria who?"

"Maria Cosway. I've mentioned her to you, I know. The woman Jefferson met in France. In Paris, when he was minister, it was in the summer of seventeen eighty-six; they met through Trumbull — you know, John Trumbull, the American painter. He was a painter too — Richard Cosway, that is, her husband — and very well known in all the, uh, quote best circles. He was a member of the Royal Academy, principal painter to the Prince of Wales, all that sort of thing. And Maria Cosway, she was *something!* Young, beautiful, talented, very feminine — the works. *And* a harpsichordist, and a composer of sorts, too. That appealed to Jefferson, of course; he was very fond of music, you know. Haydn, Handel, Pergolesi, that crowd. He was a good violinist, too. Played in a string quartet when he was a student at William and Mary. Was very good, apparently. Till he broke his wrist."

"Mrs. Cosway. Maria Cosway. It's a beautiful name . . . Was Jefferson in love with her?"

"That's a good question." Raymond ran his fingers through his hair, still damp from the shower. "And it's a hard one to answer. Yes, I guess so, I expect he *was* in love with Maria Cosway."

"But didn't you say somewhere — maybe it's in your book, no, it was a lecture I heard you give somewhere, soon after we were married, I think — didn't you say that

Jefferson wasn't really interested in women? Except his wife, that is? And that after her death he never . . ."

"Yes, I did say that. But I've . . . I've changed my mind since then. Since reading Dorsey's book." Raymond paused and studied the tips of his fingers. "Maria Cosway was a remarkable woman. It's hard to say exactly what I feel about all this. Jefferson wasn't really, how shall I put it, I guess you'd just have to say he wasn't really a very sexy man. And he had some very strict ideas and beliefs about right and wrong, virtue and vice, all that . . . And Maria, as I said, she was a beauty, and young — just in her middle twenties when they met, fifteen or sixteen years younger than Cosway. As for Cosway himself, he was a notorious, uh, philanderer. A sort of grotesque little guy, too. It wasn't what you'd call an ideal marriage."

Again Raymond paused and waved his hands.

"Maria really bowled him over, I guess. And he her, I'd say. They were both, I guess you'd have to say, ready for each other. But I used to think that nothing ever came of it."

"Used to think? What do you mean?"

"I'm not really sure. It's obvious from their letters that Maria really turned Jefferson on. Drove him right up the wall, that sort of thing. But, after all, she *was* married . . . and there was something in his nature . . . As I said, Jefferson just wasn't a sexy man. Not prudishness; God knows, he was no prig. You have to think of him in terms of eighteenth-century America, not France . . . I don't know. He just couldn't let himself go . . . the way Franklin did, for example."

Again Raymond paused and rubbed his nose reflectively. "But there're some recent historians, they say just the opposite. A woman on the West Coast, Berkeley or U.C.L.A., I can't remember which, name of Willoughby — Professor Snow Willoughby, she's writing what her publishers call an *intimate* biography of Jefferson; she believes, or says she believes, that Maria was Jefferson's mistress. Categorically. Just like that."

"Hmmm! I never heard that when I was going to school in Howard County, Ohio." Margaret walked to the window, and gazed for a moment at the slowly darkening lake. "Whatever became of her? Of *them?*"

"Nothing really. They saw each other a lot, maybe they were lovers, but I find that hard to believe. Then finally, Jefferson had to come home — this was in the fall of seventeen eighty-nine — to be Washington's secretary of state." Raymond shook his head and half closed his eyes. "Far as I know, they never saw each other again . . . but I expect Professor Willoughby in California may have some ideas about that, too. Jefferson wrote Maria an incredible sort of letter several months after he'd been back in America; he wrote her secretly, incidentally, sent letters through friends or if he had to use the regular postal service he never signed his name and all that sort of thing. He said, in French by the way, that he'd heard that she was pregnant." Again he shook his head. "I expect someone will try to prove that he was the father, but the dates don't fit and besides there's nothing in any later letters even to suggest it. And anyhow, that just wasn't Jefferson's style."

"Hmmm! And then?"

"Nothing really. They did write to each other; he

kept talking about wanting to see her and I think she'd
have come to America if he'd really *asked* her to, but I
have the feeling he didn't want to. He was afraid or something, couldn't let himself go. They're very sad letters;
you should read them. They were discovered just a few
years ago. Jefferson's favorite grandson had kept them
hidden; they're in Dorsey's book."

"And *was* there a child?"

"Yeah, a little girl; she died when she was five or six.
Cosway was beastly about it."

"Ugh!"

"You can say that again. After that, Maria had some
crazy affairs, I guess you'd call them; one of them was
with a singer, I can't remember his name; he was a well-
known male soprano."

"My goodness!"

"And later she was in and out of convents, and somewhere along the line she founded some sort of convent
school, the college of, uh, Santa Maria della Grazie or
something of the sort. In Italy; I forgot to say she'd been
born in Italy. Her parents were English; the old man was
a wealthy merchant . . . Well, Cosway died, finally, on
July fourth, incidentally! And Maria lived to be very
old, till the late eighteen thirties, ten, twelve years, it must
have been, after Jefferson died. All this is in Dorsey's
book; get her to tell you about it. You'll enjoy talking
with her; she has some interesting ideas about Maria."

"It's a very sad story, terribly sad. But enormously interesting. Maria, I mean. And Dorsey Jack Morgan too,"
she added hastily. "What else has she done?"

"Dorsey's a good editor." Raymond looked at the clock

on the bed table and whistled softly. "It's getting late, we'd better hurry." He placed his drink on the marble windowsill before carefully removing his new dinner jacket from a plastic garment bag.

"Those lapels are a little wide," he muttered, and turned to her. "Dorsey's not the greatest writer in the world, but she's a first-rate editor. She's been working on a collection of Jefferson's letters to his children. They're very interesting, those letters. They show him, and his daughters, too, in a different light from, uh, the traditional nineteenth-century biographers like Randall. Particularly the ones to his favorite daughter. Martha Jefferson Randolph. Her husband was Thomas Mann Randolph; he was Governor of Virginia, you know; he was an interesting man, but as wild as a buck. They had eleven children; one of them, the oldest, Jeff — for Jefferson, of course — was the one who concealed the Jefferson-Cosway letters; he was Jefferson's executor. Martha, she's the most complex member of the family, except for Jefferson himself, of course. Get Dorsey to tell you about Martha sometime. She's planning to do a book about her, after she finishes editing the letters. Martha — Patsy, Jefferson called her — she had *her* problems, too: ran away from Randolph and — "

"Ran away! I never heard that at school, either."

Raymond smiled as he carefully laid out his dinner jacket on the bed. "There're a lot of things you didn't hear about at school, Mrs. Green." He stared at his reflection in the mirror and ran his fingers across cheeks and chin, his face suddenly serious, so serious that Margaret hastened to his side.

"Are you all right, Ray? What's the matter? Why are you staring at yourself that way?"

"I'm getting fat, baby." Ruefully he stroked his cheeks before glancing downward at his stomach. "Look at that belly! How would you like being married to a fat man?"

"I'd love it. Do you know where I can find one? But he must be a Jefferson scholar. And a member of the Mafia, to coin a phrase. And he must know why Martha Jefferson Randolph ran away from her husband. *And* Maria Cosway. And Sally . . . what did you say her name was, the slave at Monticello, the one you said you did the article on . . . ?"

"Sally Hemings. Black Sally."

Margaret grimaced. "Pardon my Yankee prejudices, but I hate that name." Suddenly very serious, she put her arms around him and hugged him. "And above all, his name must be Raymond Green. I'd love you even if I had to pull you around in a little red wagon. Or even a big one. But not now, we'd really better hurry. Keep talking, though, while I'm doing my hair. Tell me more so I can impress the Mafia."

"You'd better ask Dorsey; she knows a lot more about this than I do. And I expect you're right, we *had* better hurry, sure enough. Have you seen my tie? My black bow tie?"

Hairbrush in hand, Margaret hesitated, and looked dubiously at the dinner jacket. "Your black tie? I think I saw it there, near your coat. But why . . . ?"

"Ah, good. You know I haven't worn evening clothes but once or twice since we've been married. Don't have many occasions for it at our prairie home, do we?"

"Not many." She paused at the door to the bathroom. "But, dear, is it, I mean, do you think it's, well, appropriate?"

"What's that?" Tie in his hands, Raymond stared at the slowly closing door. "I can't quite hear you."

"Nothing, dear . . . What else has Dorsey done?"

"That's about it, the Cosway book and the letters. Why?"

"That doesn't sound like very much."

"It isn't very much. I never really said she'd done very much. But" — Raymond's voice was unusually mild — "I guess Armistead may have had something to do with her getting the invitation."

"Armistead!" Margaret's voice rose half an octave. "My goodness, I'm dying to meet Armistead!"

"He'll be at dinner tonight. You'll like him."

"Ray?"

"Uh-huh?"

"Did anything ever . . . ever go on between Armistead and Dorsey Jack Morgan? Is that what Craig meant at the airport when he said he was worried about Armistead? What he wanted to talk with you about?"

"What made you think that?"

She opened the bathroom door and stuck her head out. "Women's intuition, I guess. And you did say once that Armistead had been . . . I think you used the term a cocksman or something similar."

"Surely, madam" — Raymond's brow was furrowed in mock gravity — "you jest."

"No, honestly, that's what you said."

"I don't remember saying that." He stared at himself

in the mirror, fumbling with the tie before pulling it from his collar and in mild exasperation laying it on the dresser. "I don't remember, Meg, but maybe I did say that. Armistead's always been a very handsome man, honey, still is, as a matter of fact; women have, uh, always been important to him. And Helen . . . you'll understand when you meet her. She's nice, in a way, that is, but I wouldn't think she'd have been much fun to live with all these years. And . . ." Raymond's voice trailed away faintly.

"What *about* Helen?"

Raymond lifted his hands in helpless supplication. "Well, she's a little on the cold side; slightly balmy, too. And she's a very proud woman, almost arrogant, you might say. She grew up on the Lawn, that sort of thing — her father was Dean of the Medical School here and Helen was a med student when she met Armistead. I expect maybe Helen gave Armistead a hard time, now and then: *his* father was a high-school teacher from near Danville. I guess her family didn't quite approve of Armistead."

"And Dorsey Jack? What about Dorsey Jack Morgan and Armistead?"

"Well" — Raymond reached for his tie — "she *was* Armistead's research assistant once."

Margaret sniffed suspiciously. "Research assistant!"

"That's right, Meg. Research assistant." He waved his tie helplessly. "I'm having a rough time with this, honey. Help me with it, will you?"

Margaret hesitated, glancing from the tie to the dinner jacket.

"What's the matter? What are you smiling for?"

"Don't be irritated." Again she looked from the tie to the dinner jacket. "Are you sure you won't be irritated?"

Raymond grinned. "You know if there's anything that irritates me it's for someone to tell me not to be irritated. Okay, I give up. I won't be irritated. What's the matter?"

"Don't think I'm being critical, Ray, but do you think a dinner jacket's really . . . appropriate?"

The phone on the bed table suddenly buzzed; saved by the bell, Margaret thought, as she reached for the receiver.

"Ray?" The voice was soft as the spring air when they had driven from the Charlottesville airport.

"This is Mrs. Green, just a minute, please." Margaret was suddenly conscious of her own Middle Western *r*'s. "I'll — "

Before she could continue, the owner of the voice introduced herself, welcomed her to Charlottesville, and asked her and Raymond to *jawn* them for drinks downstairs; of course, Margaret heard herself saying in a decidedly cool voice, how very nice, yes, we'd like to, and the receiver clicked in her ear.

"That was *Dawsee Jack Mawgann*," she said. "Professor Davis's *research assistant*. We're being awaited, *uhwayatid*, that is, in the Fahlstaff Room."

Raymond paused in the act of pulling on a pair of gray flannel trousers. "Can it, baby. Dorsey's a good person, you'll like her." He nodded toward the dinner jacket which he had replaced in its plastic garment bag, and looked at her sheepishly. "You were right, honey. Give me a hand with this, will you?"

She patted the shoulders of the dark gray Harris-tweed

jacket, conservative like the dinner clothes newly purchased for the trip to Charlottesville.

"It looks fine, Ray, just fine. You cut quite a *figga'*, Professor."

He squinted as he put his arm around her waist.

"Don't try to soft-soap me, *Miz* Green. *You* look wonderful, I'm prideful for you." He placed his glasses carefully in his breast pocket. "To the Falstaff Room . . . and the Mafia."

At the door to the elevator, Margaret hesitated before quickly kissing his forehead. "Onward and upward with the arts, right?"

He smiled and raised both loosely clenched fists, thumbs upward.

"Just one thing, honey: how did he do it?"

"Do it? Do what? Who, for God's sake? What are you talking about?"

"Thomas Jefferson, of course. His wrist. How did Thomas Jefferson break his wrist?"

CHAPTER 3

A QUIET DRINK AMONG FRIENDS
AND ACQUAINTANCES

Their [University of Virginia students]
drink at all times water, a young stomach
needing no stimulating drinks, and the
habit of using them being dangerous.
Thomas Jefferson to Mr. Laporte, June
4, 1819

As they approached the Falstaff Room, Raymond paused and turned to Margaret.

"He was jumping over a stile. To impress Maria, apparently. They were on a picnic or something of the sort, shortly after they'd met. The wrist was improperly set. It gave him trouble the rest of his life."

"That's Calvinism in action for you, all right. But it's a nice story, in a way; it makes him seem so . . . so human."

Raymond nodded and glanced upward. The pediment to the massive pair of walnut doors was elaborately ornamented with arabesques of grape leaves, cherubs' heads, and assorted fruits and vegetables; above it leered a larger-than-life boar's head. Shaking his shoulders as though to loosen a cramped muscle, he returned the leer and, one hand on the brass doorknob, smiled at Margaret. "He was a human being all right."

Inside and narrowing his eyes in the muted amber light from a scattering of recessed electric candles, Raymond fumbled for Margaret's hand.

"Dark as a wolf's mouth — " he began, but his comment was interrupted by a gentle voice from a far corner of the room.

"Raymond! Raymond Green!"

Margaret checked what would have been an audible gasp. What she had been anticipating she hardly knew. Not the fat little mouse with heavy bifocals and ink-smudged stubby fingers that Raymond's first comments about the archivist had conjured up. A drudge? A little old lady in tennis shoes? Or — engendered perhaps by Raymond's slightly defensive attitude toward the archivist — a Twiggy or Raquel Welch? Nothing had prepared her for the tall woman who approached them like some treasure-laden diver slowly surfacing toward sunlight and sky. In the dim light Miss Morgan seemed to have the face of a Botticelli angel, a pale provocative face topped by carefully contoured ash-colored hair. Except for her height — she was at least half a head taller than Raymond — the archivist was as beautiful as any woman Margaret had ever seen, with a beauty enhanced by an unusual breadth and purity of brow and clarity of eye. Her body appeared as lovely as her face; it moved with such mysterious liquidity that Margaret, who knew her poetry, was reminded of Robert Herrick's "Upon Julia's Clothes." She wore a dinner dress so unobtrusively elegant that Margaret speculated momentarily on the appropriateness of her own.

"Margaret, dear. How very good it is to meet you." Miss Morgan smiled warmly at Margaret, placed her hands on Raymond's shoulders, and lightly kissed him on each cheek. "We've heard so much about you. But come, do sit down. It's drinking time, you know."

She took Margaret's hand in her own — warm and soft,

Margaret reflected with mixed emotions — and led her toward a large corner table, Raymond following discreetly a step or two behind. Fogel Freiberg remained seated while his companion, a tall stooped man in tweeds with a ravaged face and imposing grenadier mustaches, rose unsteadily but smiling, his eyes magnified behind the heavy lenses of his Ben Franklin glasses.

"I'm Thorpe Taliaferro, Mrs. Green, an old friend of your husband's."

His voice, though not unpleasant, was so slurred that Margaret could scarcely hear him; it seemed to come from far away, as though it had risen slowly from the depths of a long-abandoned well. He bowed slowly, his oblong head drifting toward one angular shoulder, before extending a bony hand to Raymond. "Good to see you, Ray, it's been a long time."

"And have you all met Mr. Freiberg? Fogel Freiberg? The editor of *Native Roots*?"

"My favorite poopsheet." Taliaferro's voice was barely audible. "Hist'ry for the masses."

"Yes, we all came in from the airport together." Anticipating a possible grumble from Raymond or Freiberg, Margaret quickly sat down beside the dark little man.

"That's right, we all came in with Craig. And you're right, Thorpe, it has been a long time. When was it? At those meetings in Williamsburg? Five years ago, or was it six?"

"Five, Ray." Miss Morgan's voice, though gentle, was authoritative. "But do sit down, Ray. I expect you and Margaret are tired after your trip."

Thorpe Taliaferro, after folding his long body clumsily
into the chair beside Margaret, started to speak but Fogel
Freiberg had cleared his throat and turned his melancholy
eyes upon her.

"Miss Morgan was just telling us you're a novelist, Mrs.
Green. Or is it Ms? You're Women's Lib, maybe?"

At the comparative gentleness of the poet's voice Margaret was momentarily taken aback. "Women's Lib? No,
not really, but yes, in a way, that is. I'm not sure that
either the Mailers or the Milletts have the right answers."
Was she imagining it or was Thorpe Taliaferro mumbling
something that sounded like "Mailer's a flailer but Millett
will kill it"? He's stoned, she realized suddenly, absolutely stoned. "And I'm hardly a novelist, but thank you
very much, Dorsey, you're very generous. I've done one
mystery and've just about finished another — suspense
novels, I'd rather call them — but I'm hardly a novelist."

"Nonsense." Raymond's voice was neither truculent nor
conciliatory but a little of each. "She's a fine novelist, Freiberg."

She smiled at her husband across the table but in mild
embarrassment, as though trying to say "Thank you, dear,
thank you very much, but please . . ."

"I expect you're right, Green." Freiberg swung his
large head toward Raymond. "I'm quite sure you're absolutely right."

How like a bull he is, swinging his head at Ray that way,
Margaret thought, a very small, very aggressive little bull,
defiant, uncertain, afraid. She felt a surge of sympathy for
the little man, the sort of feeling one might have for a
homely, unliked but talented child.

"Do you write under your own name?" Freiberg was saying. "I'd like to read some of your work."

"No," Margaret began, but the querulous voice of Thorpe Taliaferro interrupted her.

"I need 'notha' drink, Dorsey; where's that l'il freak with the drinks?"

"Of course, Thorpe. And what will you have, Margaret? Bourbon on the rocks for you, Ray?"

Miss Morgan beckoned the mini-skirted waitress in the Betsy Ross cap, but before she could catch her eye a beaming Craig Babcock was broad-shouldering his way across the floor, followed by a slender elderly woman of indeterminate age and her husband, a man whom Margaret instinctively recognized as Armistead Davis; neither he nor Craig, she noted with satisfaction, wore dinner clothes. Magnificently white-haired, with searching blue eyes beneath still-black eyebrows and skin the color of light saddle leather, Armistead Davis was all that Raymond had prepared her for and more.

From the moment Armistead sat down, following a warm embrace for Miss Morgan and an equally jovial clasping of Raymond's hand, the conversation eddied and swirled as rapidly as the drinks, and even Fogel Freiberg's harsh features seemed to relax and soften. Helen Davis, on the other hand, showed no inclination to participate beyond an occasional nod that to Margaret seemed distinctly condescending; beneath her faded beauty she had the taut lined skin of a woman apparently at least a decade older than her ebullient and athletic-appearing husband.

"Umm." Craig Babcock cleared his throat during a lull

in the talk. "Look what I have with me." He hoisted his enormous body from the depths of his chair and from somewhere beneath his suit coat withdrew a large book which he presented with a flourish to Armistead Davis.

"Your new book, sir. An advance copy of *Jefferson: The Rise to Power*. It arrived special delivery just before I left Monticello to pick you and Mrs. Davis up." Beaming broadly, he waved one massive arm. "I've been hoping against hope it'd get here in time. Ain't it a beauty?"

"By God!" Armistead Davis tamped out his cigarette with one hand and with the other held the book aloft. Margaret caught a glimpse of a bewigged Jefferson against a backdrop of classical columns. Armistead removed the jacket, expertly ran his fingers across the cover, opened the book, and scrutinized the title page; only then did the frown fade from his handsome face.

"There was a typo on the title page of my first book," he said to Margaret. "Something said to happen only once in a million times." He shuddered. "My name on a book for the first time. Misspelled! I've been apprehensive ever since." He patted the book as one would a favorite dog, and smiled at Craig. "How great that you could get hold of a copy so soon! I wasn't expecting it. By God, I'm delighted! Here, you all, take a look." He leaned across the table, almost upsetting Fogel Freiberg's bloody mary in the process — "Sorry about that, Fogel" — and passed it to Dorsey Jack Morgan.

"It's beautiful, Armistead, simply beautiful." The archivist leaned forward as though to embrace him, hesitated, and sank back in her chair. "Isn't it beautiful, Helen?"

Mrs. Davis nodded, smiled a thin smile, and handed the book to Raymond.

"Ummmmm." Unthinkingly he stroked the solid heft of it with admiring fingers. *What a wonderful thing a new book is how good it smells and feels so solid so palpable a manifestation of everything that went into its making from the first fumbling beginnings the months or years of research the endless grubbing around in libraries the painful mornings when everything goes wrong the blank page in the typewriter becoming a threat a menace the dreary drafts the inept writing and banal thinking the painful self-distrust am I any good am I kidding myself am I wasting my time should I have stayed at Woodberry to teach history to schoolboys and coach the boxing team but then there were the good mornings the exciting ones when everything jells ideas seem to flow rapidly from finger tips to typewriter keys and the pages accumulate and then finally magically after all the revising and all the rewriting somehow it's done finished the manuscript mailed off accepted copy-edited and then the last act the dreary proofreading from then on it's out of my hands no longer mine really but a book something I created . . .*

"Come on, Ray, keep it movin'." Thorpe Taliaferro's voice, Margaret thought, was more testy than necessary, and she started to reach out and touch Raymond's elbow, but he was shaking his head as though clearing his vision.

"It's a fine book, Arm'stead." He raised the book aloft, much in the manner of Armistead, pointing to the photograph of the author on the back jacket: Rhodes Scholar, National Book Award–winner, Bancroft Award–winner.

"It's a great book. Let's drink to Arm'stead. To *Jef-fa'son: The Rise to Powa'*. But most of all to our fren', our good fren'."

Good Lord, thought Margaret, Ray sounds half-smashed too; this isn't like him, he usually tends to take a back seat, it must have been the plane ride. Then they were rising to their feet, laughing and talking. All but Thorpe Taliaferro, she noted with some surprise. After making a slight effort the bibliographer had slumped back in his chair; and she heard the single monosyllable *balls,* unnoticed by the others in the general confusion, the scraping of chairs, and the hubbub of conversation.

"That husband of yours is something else." Armistead leaned across the table and looked at Margaret with feigned seriousness. "I hadn't realized he was such an orator." He drained his glass, muttered "Delicious," and nodded to Dorsey Jack Morgan, who with a slim finger summoned the waitress. "But I always knew he had talent." He smiled, his voice alive with genuine good nature and friendship. "Raymond the Good. He was one of the best students I ever had, you know. Indeed, perhaps *the* best of the younger members of our little Mafia."

"How nice of you to say that. How very nice."

"Nice, nothin'. It's the truth. Wait till that second book of his comes out. How's it coming along, Ray? Have you ever decided what Jefferson really thought of Richard Cosway's paintings? Craig, you've seen some of the manuscript, haven't you? Or you, Fogel? And where's your beautiful wife, incidentally?"

Before they could reply, Armistead inhaled deeply,

coughed, and ground out his cigarette before turning to Helen Davis, who had remained virtually silent since their entrance, occasionally moistening her lips with a discreet sip from her glass.

"Did you bring one of my holders, dear? Helen rations me, you know. And she makes me use a holder — after my first two packs of the day."

"Not very successfully, I'm afraid." Mrs. Davis withdrew a long F.D.R. cigarette holder from her brocaded handbag and passed it to Armistead, who inserted and carefully lighted a cigarette almost as long as the holder and again turned to Craig.

"What about it, Craig, what do you think of it?"

"Haven't seen it; my old roommate hasn't deigned to show me the manuscript."

"You'll like it," Armistead said as Raymond made vague, apologetic sounds. "Best thing that's been done on Jefferson's intellectual int'rests; beats all that New York crowd all hollow."

Absent-mindedly he reached for his empty glass. "What's holding up that little nymphet, Dorsey? Let's have drinks for the Greens, please, ma'am; drinks for the young scholars from out of the West. Ah, there she is; bless you, child."

"Is it *that* good?" Freiberg's whisper was incredulous. "Your husband's manuscript?"

"I haven't seen it. Ray never shows me anything he's writing till it's finished. He's — I guess you'd have to say he's very superstitious. But it's essentially a character study and, as Mr. Davis just said, about Jefferson's intellectual interests. Ray's more concerned with Jefferson's personal life than his public career — with his ideas and his reading and . . ."

Thorpe Taliaferro leaned forward, ashes from his cigarette falling into Fogel Freiberg's bloody mary. "Had a canine appetite for reading, Jeffa'son." For a moment he gazed myopically into Margaret's bosom. "Thass his own phrase, thass pretty good izzen it?"

"Yes." Raymond's voice sounded only slightly irritated. "That's a very good, uh, phrase."

Muttering, the librarian again leaned forward as though to respond, but Armistead Davis was raising his glass. "Let's all drink to Ray's new book. The best student I eva' had. To the scholar-boxer."

As they rose to their feet, Fogel Freiberg leaned toward Margaret; his hair, which during the drive from the airport had writhed as though charged with electricity, was meticulously brushed, and there was about the poet the slight and pleasant scent of mild tobacco and English Leather cologne; she resisted the impulse to pat the head so close to hers. "What is this?" he was whispering loudly. "A mutual admiration society? Or an ex-athletes' reunion? *This* is a group of scholars? I thought we were here because of Jefferson."

Armistead Davis carefully replaced his glass on the table. "Eh? What's that, Fogel? I didn't quite hear you."

The poet smiled blandly. "I was just saying to Mrs. Green that all of you academic jocks seem to stick together."

"What do you mean, academic jocks?"

"You, sir" — Freiberg paused as Armistead fumbled for a fresh cigarette, an amused smile on his ruddy face — "as my informants have briefed me, still hold the Virginia long-jump record. A remarkable achievement. And Mr. Babcock was a reasonably good football player."

"So?" At the truculence in Raymond's voice, Miss Morgan leaned forward and gently tugged his coattail.

"And I believe, Green, you were not only a boxer but a Southern Conference champion." Freiberg ran his tongue over his front teeth as though removing an unpleasant aftertaste.

Margaret blinked: That husband of mine!

"Well, so what?" Raymond was smiling but there was an edge to his voice.

"Oh, but you were so beautiful, Ray!" Dorsey Jack Morgan smiled at Freiberg and Raymond, and turned to a surprised Margaret as the tension slowly diminished. "You should have seen him, Margaret. They were so beautiful, all of the boys on the boxing team. In their white shorts and the dark blue shirts with V-I-R-G-I-N-I-A in orange across them. And, Ray, you were the most beautiful of them all." She lowered her contralto voice incongruously. "The announcer would say . . . how does it go? In this corner, weighing in at . . . how much was it?"

"A hundred and sixty or a hundred and fifty-eight, usually." Self-consciously Raymond glanced downward at his stomach. "I was a middleweight then."

"Weighing in at one hundred and sixty pounds. In this corner, for the University of Virginia." Again the archivist turned toward Margaret. "Oh, you would have loved it! Boxing was *the* sport at the University in those days, much bigger than football or basketball. And Ray always looked so serious. All the boys were serious, but Raymond most of all. Grim Green, they used to call him."

A ripple of laughter flowed around the table, eddied, and flowed again.

"Grim Green." Margaret spread her hands in mock bewilderment, pleased but somewhat put off by the affectionate tone of Dorsey's reminiscences. "He never told me *that*. He *did* say something about 'having boxed' or something of the sort. But a Southern Conference champion!" She smiled. "Grim Green. What a nickname!"

"We were reading Graham Greene at the time," Miss Morgan volunteered. "In James Southall Wilson's course in the English novel. The sports editor of *College Topics* was in the class that year, too, and he thought it up. What was the Greene novel we read that time, Ray? *Brighton Rock?*"

"No, not *Brighton Rock*." Raymond's voice was surprisingly authoritative. Thank Heavens, Margaret thought, he's not really smashed after all. "It was *The Powa' and the Glory*. It came out the second year I was, uh, boxing." Abruptly, as though he had overstepped an invisible boundary line, he paused, looked around the table in some embarrassment, and quickly finished his drink.

That Raymond! An historian and a boxing champion taking a course in the English novel. This is one of the so-nice things about a second marriage: one keeps learning so many things. But as Dorsey Jack Morgan inclined her beautiful head toward Raymond and seemed about to whisper in his ear, Margaret's euphoria vanished. "It's a good novel, but I liked *Brighton Rock* better," Margaret announced tartly, surprised at the asperity of her voice.

"I haven't read either of them." Having disposed of the matter, Armistead Davis smiled at the occupants of the table and turned to Freiberg. "But you're absolutely right, Fogel. We jocks, as you say, do stick together."

"Dorsey . . ." Thorpe Taliaferro's plaintive voice drifted away, unheard, unnoticed.

"But I wasn't aware that our exploits were so . . . so well remembered. And I didn't know you were a sports buff."

"A sports buff I'm not." There was no warmth in the poet's voice. "One of the girls in my research department dug that up for me."

"Oh?"

"Fogel is here to write an article about all this." Craig Babcock waved his huge hands helplessly. "For *Native Roots*."

"Is he, though? I hadn't heard that. I hope you won't be disappointed, Fogel."

"Disappointed?" The poet raised one shoulder in a gesture so Madison Avenue that Margaret with difficulty suppressed a smile. "No, I'm sure I won't be disappointed, Professor Davis."

"Good!" Armistead glanced at Taliaferro who, muttering, had removed his glasses and was absently running his fingers through the drooping ends of his mustache. "But let's drop the professor bit, shall we? And, Dorsey" — he fumbled in his pocket for a cigarette — "you're far too young to give up smoking. Won't you have one? Guaranteed to be one hundred per cent tobacco-free. And I think our friend Freiberg is ready for a drink."

"*I* think it's about time we went to dinner." Helen Davis's faint voice was as dry as sandpaper.

Freiberg hesitated, before bleakly examining the ashes floating in the remains of his bloody mary. "Another drink I could use. If Mrs. Davis, that is . . ."

"My glasses, damn it, my glasses, Dorsey." Thorpe Taliaferro's bony fingers rummaged impotently through the clutter on the table.

"What else did you say you found, Fogel?"

The poet's dark eyes flickered from Armistead to Helen Davis. "I didn't say, actually. But since you ask, it was, oh, things about Mrs. What's-her-name; you know, the one he met in France."

"Mrs. Cosway? Maria Cosway? Is that who you mean?"

Freiberg grinned. "That's right, Mrs. Cosway. That's the very one." He closed his eyes as though in deep thought. "And then there's that other one. I can't remember her name either. My mind, I must be losing it." He opened his eyes and rubbed his forehead. "You know, the woman at Monticello, the one they call Black Sally. The one everybody's been so interested in lately."

"Sally Hemings?" There was, suddenly, a hard edge to Armistead Davis's voice. "Is that who you mean?"

"That's it. Sally Hemings." The poet paused dramatically. "The half-sister of Jefferson's wife. His mistress."

In the sudden silence the drumming of Craig Babcock's huge fingers sounded like rain on a tin roof.

"That's not so! All that talk. It's nothing but — but a lot of Yankee scandal-mongering."

As though suddenly aware of the vehemence in his voice the curator paused, looked around the table, and again waved his hands helplessly. "Sorry, Fogel. You . . . you have every right to your opinion, of course. I just don't believe that garbage myself. It's possible, anything's possible. There was even a story in one of the papers recently, just a few months ago, you may have seen it, that John F. Kennedy's still alive. On that island, you know, Onassis's? I can't remember the name. A fisherman or somebody said he was wheeled out on the terraces, every day, a vegetable." He shook his head slowly. "Even *that's* possible, I guess. But Jefferson and Sally Hemings. No sir! And it's no great discovery, anyhow. From Callender to all those — those jokers out on the West Coast, people have always spread misinformation about Jefferson." Again the curator shook his great head. "Slander, lies, abuse. There was even an article about it in one of the Sunday supplements, not so long ago."

His voice trailed away, and he looked toward Armistead as though for affirmation; the biographer started to speak but was interrupted by Helen Davis, her eyes contemptuous.

"Do you have any evidence for your remarks, sir?" Her voice was as cold as her eyes.

"Evidence? No, Mrs. Davis, I have no evidence. I was only asking. Asking for information."

Armistead glanced at Helen who, tightlipped, continued to glare at Freiberg. "It's quite probable that Mrs.

Jefferson and Sally Hemings had the same father; I have
a few things to say about that myself tomorrow night. But
Craig's quite right, Freiberg. That business has been
kicked around for a long long time, almost ever since the
death of his wife."

"My glasses, damn it." Thorpe Taliaferro pounded the
table and Raymond, after a quick survey, bent down to
search the floor. Freiberg muttered, "Ah I see Tom Rover
is doing his thing"; Craig Babcock placed his head in both
hands and closed his eyes; and Helen Davis half rose from
her chair, her voice controlled but hostility evident in the
set of her chin and the stiffness of her body.

"It's time we leave for dinner."

"I expect, dear, you're right; it *is* about time. But Mr.
Freiberg had started to say something about Mrs. Cosway.
What was it, Fogel?"

"Mrs. Cosway, she was a very interesting person."

Raymond's head suddenly emerged from beneath the
table. "Very complex. Almost schizoid. So was Martha
Jefferson. His daughter, that is, not his wife."

The poet regarded Raymond as though for the first time
becoming aware that an ex-boxer could be a reasoning human being. "For Martha Jefferson, that's the word. Schizoid." Again he closed his eyes, shrugging theatrically.
"That interest in Daddy!"

"Oh, come off it!"

"Come off what, Craig?" The poet's eyes twinkled, but
his voice was innocent.

"Oh . . ." Craig Babcock shrugged his heavy shoulders
and again looked at Armistead beseechingly.

"You're covering a lot of territory, Fogel. But let's forget Martha. What were you about to say about Maria Cosway?"

Freiberg regarded Armistead Davis quizzically before replying, a slight smile playing around the corners of his mouth. "Is it true that Mrs. Cosway came to Washington? When Jefferson was Vice President? No pun intended. Under cover, of course."

"What in God's name?" Armistead shook his head in disbelief as Raymond emerged hastily from beneath the table.

"Mrs. Cosway in Washington? What is this, some kind of joke?"

"Ridiculous!" Craig Babcock's voice was incredulous. "Freiberg, you amaze me. What are you up to anyhow?"

"Like I said, I have a superb research assistant. She — "

"My glasses!" Thorpe Taliaferro again pounded the table. "Get my glasses, someone, damn it." Suddenly he rose to his feet, swaying and making wild, windmilling movements with both lanky arms, and staggered toward Freiberg.

"J'accuse!" His voice, like his long outstretched index finger, was mockingly menacing.

"What in thunder?"

At the sound of Armistead Davis's voice Taliaferro wheeled, and continued the wild motions.

"J'accuse you, too!"

"Come on, Thorpe, knock it off." Raymond, stepping around the table nimbly, confronted the swaying figure of the bibliographer.

"J'accuse you too, Ray."

Mrs. Davis rose haughtily from the table. "*I* am leaving."

"You're absolutely right, my dear." Armistead offered Helen his arm, hesitated, and took another look at Taliaferro, who still towered above Raymond, one bony finger upraised. Armistead's shoulders began to shake; face flushed, he struggled to gain control of himself, but finally doubled over, bursting into laughter. And then they were all laughing, all but Helen Davis, and Taliaferro, who regarded the scene with bewilderment for a long moment before sinking into his chair. His laughter finally contained, Armistead again offered Helen his arm and together they started from the room. A few steps from the door he turned slowly.

"It's not as wild as it sounds, folks. But, Fogel, how in thunder . . . ?"

"I'll tell you about that some time, Professor Davis. I mean Armistead."

"I'd appreciate that. And, Fogel, will Mrs. Freiberg be joining us for dinner?"

"I — I'm not sure. I'll have to go see." The poet gestured vaguely, hesitating a moment too long, it seemed to Margaret. "We had a long wait at La Guardia. She's slightly under the weather. I'm afraid she may not be able to make it."

"Too bad. Do hope she can. Please to pay our respects if she can't, will you? Shall we go, Helen?"

Freiberg watched them leave, then turned to Craig Babcock. "I'll go upstairs and see. I'll be right back."

"Good. If we're not here, meet us out in front."

Freiberg nodded and, running his fingers through his twisted curls, hastened from the table, almost bumping into the waitress. Near the door he turned toward Margaret and Raymond and raised his right hand, the first and second fingers forming the peace sign. Is he smiling or smirking, Margaret wondered; then she decided he was smiling and started to respond in kind, but the poet had already turned again and was hastening from the Falstaff Room.

CHAPTER 4

CONVERSATION AND REFLECTIONS AT MIDNIGHT

There is a natural aristocracy among men. The grounds of this are virtue and talents . . . There is also an artificial aristocracy, founded on wealth and birth, without either virtue or talents . . . natural aristocracy I consider as the most precious gift of nature . . . Thomas Jefferson to John Adams, October 28, 1813

"I REALLY DIDN'T LIKE the Eppeses, darling," Margaret said aloud, more to herself than to Raymond, who was again in the shower. "I like everybody else, even Helen Davis, but not the Eppeses, particularly Carla; was she always that bitchy?"

She sat at the window of their room at the Boar's Head, brushing her hair almost automatically and occasionally smiling at her blurred reflection in the windowpane. She felt both mildly exhilarated and pleasantly relaxed after their love-making; how wrong were the cynics who prattled about love-making as a prelude to death! What an evening it had been! Armistead Davis, so attractive and vigorous. Helen Davis, not really unpleasant even in spite of her coolness. Freiberg and Thorpe Taliaferro, what a pair they were. And Dorsey Jack Morgan! In spite of her instinctive twinges of jealousy, it was impossible not to like *her:* poor Dorsey, at this moment in the emergency room of the University hospital! But the Eppeses, they were something else again . . .

. . .

After Fogel Freiberg's sudden departure from the Falstaff Room, they had all made their way to Craig Babcock's king-sized station wagon in the courtyard of the Boar's Head. Just as they were about to leave, the poet had reappeared, without his seductive wife and having replaced what Raymond had called his Buster Brown outfit with a comparatively conservative double-breasted blue pinstripe overshadowed by a flowered tie almost as wide as it was long. Her recollection of the brief drive to Farmington was pleasantly blurred: a warm and gentle breeze from some nearby orchard had carried the scent of new blossoms through the open windows of the wagon, a few pale stars were flickering above the foothills of the Blue Ridge and the indigo outline of the Ragged Mountains, and in a brief moment of silence some premature nightbird — could it have been a mockingbird, did mockingbirds sing in Virginia in mid-April? — had flooded the air with song. Then they were stopping before Farmington with its white columns and galleries rising behind dark masses of box and yew, and the voice of Dorsey Jack Morgan quietly faded away: *What is Virginia?/Who are the Cavaliers?*

Craig Babcock was telling her that Jefferson himself had designed Farmington, and then the voice of Fogel Freiberg arose, seemingly from the very bowels of the station wagon, and she had a sudden ludicrous vision of the small poet imprisoned in the trunk — if indeed station wagons had trunks, which upon reflection she knew they did not: "I doubt that, Professor Davis, I doubt that very seriously." In the ensuing quiet, someone was saying, as though in the strictest confidence: "You know, I'd rather take a beating than see a Sidney Poitier movie," followed by Armistead Davis's ebullient: "Freiberg's absolutely

right, Ray, I'll drink to him, by God I will, but he don't
know from nuthin' about Sally Hemings or Maria Cosway . . ."

Then they were eating in the almost deserted high-ceilinged octagonal dining room, a dinner delicious and un-
eventful until the arrival of the Eppeses halfway through
the second course (a delicious crab compote in a shell of
mouth-watering pastry). A spare, vaguely aristocratic-
looking man with thinning sandy hair and a tendency to
whinny and snort, Webster Eppes was chairman of the
history department and, she knew, had been a leading
contender for the newly established Thomas Jefferson
Chair at the University; Carla, his wife, was a birdlike
individual with a pink and white chipmunk face, nervous
fingers, and a bosom astounding in so small a woman.
They had greeted each guest by turn with excessive but
vaguely patronizing cordiality, and Carla had chattered
throughout the remainder of the meal in what had seemed
to Margaret an offensively cultivated voice. After apolo-
gizing for being late, Mrs. Eppes, leaning toward Armistead Davis and almost upsetting her wine glass with one
bobbing breast, had announced that she had been out to
the "house" all morning and most of the afternoon, making final arrangements, instructing the servants from the
catering establishment, "and all *thet*." Everything was
ecks-kizzit, the house and *gyardens* had never looked more
beautiful. Then, turning to Margaret, she had inquired
whether or not she had ever been to Monticello. On a sudden impulse Margaret had shaken her head.

"But I am an admirer of Jefferson," she had added
hastily.

"Please, my deah." Carla Eppes, her breasts wobbling, had raised one fluttering hand as if to ward off a blow. "Mista' Jeffa'son. Heah we refer to Him only as Mista' Jeffa'son."

Armistead Davis had raised his eyebrows and smiled wryly at Raymond, who had smiled back. Had Webster Eppes intercepted that exchange? Margaret hoped he had not; it would mean, she felt, the end to any hopes Raymond entertained of ever being asked back to teach at the University of Virginia. And then Eppes himself had turned the conversation by asking Fogel Freiberg something about *Native Roots*; but the poet either ignored the question or had not heard it in the first place. Thorpe Taliaferro — after his spectacular performance in the Falstaff Room the Mafia had ignored the librarian; to all intents and purposes he had ceased to exist — remained silent throughout most of the meal, occasionally lifting his head long enough to consume quantities of the table wine, a Chablis so deliciously dry it sparkled upon the palate. Even Craig Babcock, as busily attentive as always, seemed somewhat less ebullient than usual, but then, Margaret knew, he had had a long day and was faced with two even longer ones before the Founder's Day activities would be climaxed with the banquet at Monticello. Dorsey Jack Morgan was her customary pleasant self, chatting with animation, and, like Thorpe Taliaferro, drinking glass after glass of the Chablis . . .

"Lots of people are writing about Jefferson nowadays," Armistead had replied to one of Margaret's questions toward the end of dinner. "More so than ever. Most of us are around here, except for some jokers on the West Coast."

"You see, Margaret," Dorsey Jack Morgan had added, "all the important Jefferson material is here at the University or at Princeton . . ."

Margaret smiled. "Yes, Julian Boyd; that's where the papers are being edited."

"Good woman!" Armistead beamed. "I see that Ray's been having you do your homework."

"And at th' Library of Congress!" Thorpe Taliaferro had broken his long silence, put down his wine glass, and turned his befuddled gaze in her direction. "Don't forget th' Library of Congress!"

"Of course, Thorpe, the Library of Congress." As always, Dorsey Jack Morgan's voice was calm, soothing, conciliatory.

"We're a very small clan," Armistead had continued without looking at the librarian, who had again slumped into his chair. "All of us" — and he had waved his hand to include everyone at the table except Fogel Freiberg — "we know each other's work, we read each other's articles and books, and as Dorsey says we're usually working at the same places so we're constantly running into each other."

He had sighed a long sigh, leaned forward, and with alcoholic gravity lowered his voice. "We know everything about each other, too much so sometimes. We even review each other's books and . . ."

"And crib each other's stuff?"

The harsh voice, of course, had been that of Fogel Frei-

berg. Although the little man was smiling genially there
was a long moment of strained silence before a ripple of
laughter eddied around the table. But Thorpe Taliaferro,
Margaret noted, was not laughing; instead a sudden flash
— irritation, amusement, hostility? — had briefly illuminated his oblong face, and Webster Eppes had made a slight
gagging sound and raised his hand toward his high forehead as though to brush away a gnat. Then the conversation had again become general and during dessert Dorsey
Jack Morgan had excused herself and walked somewhat
unsteadily from the room. Shortly afterward, they had
withdrawn to a small lounge. Liqueurs and coffee were
being served when an agitated waiter had entered, hastened to Craig Babcock, and whispered urgently in his ear.

"Good God Almighty!" Craig had leaped to his feet
and half run, half walked to the door, where he turned
and raised his huge arms in a gesture of astonishment and
despair.

"Dorsey's fallen into the swimming pool!"

* * *

At the sound of Raymond's footsteps, Margaret turned
from the window and laid her hairbrush on the bed; in
his dressing gown, still slightly bemused, his hair damp
from the shower, Raymond stood beside her, put his arms
around her, and kissed the side of her neck.

"What were you saying? I couldn't hear."

"I didn't like the Eppeses. Was Carla always that
bitchy?"

"Yeah, I guess so." Raymond frowned slightly. "Can't

say that I blame you. But nobody likes them, really. None
of the people I know. None of us."

"The people you know? You mean the Mafia?"

"Well, not *just* the Mafia. There're a lot of people who
don't think too much of Carla. Or Webster, either.
Mostly the Mafia, but a lot of good historians in general,
I'd say. Webster did do one good book, one pretty good
book, that is. Three, four years ago. *The Jeffersonian
Legacy*. It got a very good press and made a lot of money.
It's one of those big, impressive-looking books; you know,
like the Time-Life things, lots of pictures, and all that.
And it got Webster the chairmanship of the History Department at Virginia; it came out about the time that
Old Man Perkins was getting ready to retire, just the right
year for Webster. But it's not in the same class as Armistead's work or Dumas Malone's. Matter of fact, *The Jeffersonian Legacy* isn't a good book at all, I don't know
why I said it was. Webster's a hard worker, or he *was*, but
that's about all I could say for him. He *knew* the Jefferson
literature, that's for sure, but in a way his book was a
fraud."

"A fraud?"

"Well, a sort of fraud. Webster didn't have anything
new, he simply used what everybody else had done, from
the earliest Jefferson biographers to Dumas Malone and
Claude Bowers and Gilbert Chinard and Marie Kimball
and John Dos Passos and all the rest, including Armistead
and some of his graduate students, even me. He gave no
credits or acknowledgments to anybody, not even in foot-
notes. Put it all together into one big slick package and
made a lot of money on it — it was a Book-of-the-Month

selection — plus the Chairmanship. Yukkhh!"

A slight bubble of air rose in Raymond's chest and he glanced toward the bathroom.

"Did you remember the Bromo-Seltzer?"

"Yes, I did; wait here, I'll fix you some."

In the bathroom Margaret carefully measured a capful of the white granules and poured them into a glass, half filled it with tap water, and hastened back to the bedroom. "Here, drink this fast, while it's still foaming."

"Ahhh, that's better." Raymond drained the last of the bubbling liquid and placed the glass carefully on the floor by the bed. "Much better."

"So that's how Webster got as far as he has?"

Raymond stroked his chin thoughtfully. "Mostly that, anyhow. That and just by being around. Webster was always around the right people at the right time; you know that type. The Board of Visitors was always pretty high on him, too; his grandfather was chairman of the Board of Visitors years ago — Judge Eppes — and people remember things like that around here, you know. He *did* build up a good history department, I'll say that for him. And they entertained the right people, all that sort of thing; Carla was a good hostess, years ago, before she started falling apart."

He shook his head vehemently, partly in irritation, partly in amusement. " 'Please, my deah. *Mista'* Jeffa'son. Heah we refer to *Him* only as *Mista'* Jeffa'son.' " Raymond revolved his shoulders and smiled. "It was great, your saying you'd never been to Monticello . . . That Carla! She's never gotten over being married to Judge Eppes's grandson, living on the Lawn, that sort of thing.

She's originally from Clifton Fort — it's a railroad town, least attractive town in Virginia. Her father ran a junkyard or made his money in toilet seats or something of the sort."

Margaret smiled. "Oh dear, you really are a snob. You shouldn't say things like that. And it really didn't surprise me, the *Mista'* bit. I'd more or less expected that sort of thing somewhere along the way. . . . She's a real bitch, Ray, and a psycho too, I'd bet . . . Have you noticed her fingers? They're bitten . . . gnawed would be more appropriate. Down to the quick."

"No, I hadn't noticed her nails. Most men don't. Not with those . . . those udders of hers. But Carla's had some bad times. Webster's a cold fish, I expect . . . And of course everyone around here knows he's never really forgiven her for that business with Armistead."

Margaret sat upright, the hairbrush almost dropping from her hand.

"Raymond Green! What business with Armistead?"

"I thought I'd told you. Gosh, Meg, I can't remember everything." He looked at his watch and yawned portentously. "It's after twelve."

"Tell me. No going to sleep till you tell me."

"Well, it really wasn't very much. Not that I approve of that sort of thing, you know. It must have been fifteen or sixteen years ago." Raymond paused and made rapid calculations on the fingers of his left hand. "No, it was sixteen. The year Armistead was finishing his first book. *Jefferson: The Apprenticeship of a Statesman.* It won the Bancroft Award."

Margaret tapped her foot gently.

"Well, to make a long story short, Carla and Webster were spending the summer in Washington. Webster had a fellowship of some sort, he was always good at wangling money from the foundations, and Carla was helping him with his research. If you could call it that, early plumbing facilities in Albemarle County or something of that sort."

He paused and looked at Margaret.

"Did you take any?"

"Take any what?"

"Bromo-Seltzer."

"No, darling, I don't need any."

"Are you sure? You don't want to be hanging tomorrow."

"I won't be hanging tomorrow . . . I mean today. Please, Ray, forget the Bromo-Seltzer."

"Well, Carla met Armistead at the Library of Congress. In the manuscripts division. Apparently he bowled her over. Simply bowled her over. . . . That's about it, honey. I think I'll clean my teeth and hit the sack."

"That's about it, eh? Just like that. He just bowled her over, is that all?" Margaret laid her hairbrush on the table and began braiding her hair for the night. She returned to the window and gazed out at the moon-washed landscape.

"It's a shame," she said half-aloud, more to herself than to Raymond, who had returned from the bathroom, toothbrush in hand.

"What's a shame, honey?"

"Oh nothing, nothing at all."

She came to him swiftly and put her arms around him, pleasured by the strength in his arms and shoulders. "Go to bed, darling, I'll be in in a minute."

"What are you doing? What's the matter?"

"Nothing, darling, nothing at all. I just want to sit by the window a bit. Do go to bed, I'll be in in a minute."

Grumbling not uncomfortably, he made his way to the large bed, still rumpled from their love-making. Margaret pulled up the covers and switched off the light, and returned to her chair by the window.

. . .

So beautiful it was out there, so very beautiful but the Mafia   what a group of freaks!   except for Ray, and Armistead   Dorsey Jack Morgan in the emergency room of the University hospital with what probably was a broken leg   Carla and Helen Davis such a pair   and Webster Eppes and Thorpe   what is eating away at him   and that droll Fogel Freiberg baiting Armistead the way he did   he was really giving them all a hard time   their faces when he said those things about Maria Cosway and Martha Jefferson and "Daddy"   but in a way they were asking for it   even Armistead good-natured as he is and Ray too they all patronized him   I must speak to Ray about it   it must be difficult being the only Jew with all these WASPs and Craig obviously dislikes him and when he made that remark about Sally Hemings there was real hostility in his voice   I've never heard Craig speak that way to anybody   and Helen if looks could kill   "Black" Sally   I'll have to find out more from Ray about her   half-sister to Jefferson's wife   and Mauve Freiberg too I wonder where she is   and Raymond it's hard to see him in this picture   what is that statement of Mista' Jefferson's that Ray likes so much there is a natural aristocracy how does it go among men something about virtue and talent I wish I could remember it   the Mafia   I like that Armistead the great dream of Jefferson   Ray always quotes something about it   the path to wisdom ta-dum-ta-dum the will the will the will to work for men where has it fled the vision and the dream no that's Wordsworth come to the window . . .

. . .

Margaret shook herself: *tomorrow today that is will be a long day but I know I will not sleep not for a while.* Quietly she raised the window higher: so fresh the air, smelling so pleasantly, so tantalizingly, of the earth and green growing things, the soft muttering of the newly leafed beeches which surrounded the Boar's Head, and far away, far far beyond the indigo mountains: was that the cough of some night animal?

"Ray," she whispered. "Ray."

"Ummmhhhh?" The voice from the bed was sleepy, but not, she thought, too sleepy.

"Don't go to sleep yet, darling. I want to talk for a while."

Come to the window, love, sweet is the night air whither has it fled. Again she shook herself and rose quickly: I must have had too much to drink; enough of this sophomore poetry survey. She smiled and turned from the haunted landscape to creep into bed beside her husband, her hand palm downward on his bare chest, pleasured as always to feel the strong slow beat of his heart beneath the layer of softening muscle.

"Please don't go to sleep yet."

" 'S late. Too late ta talk."

"Ray, please."

"Whatta ya wanta talk about? Not Armistead an' Carla?"

Again she smiled in the darkness. How could she tell an ex-boxer, almost an hour after midnight, that she wanted to talk about Jefferson's dream and "The Forsaken Merman" and Wordsworth's Immortality Ode?

"Not really," she said. "But that's a good, um, a good substitute."

"Subs'tute? Subs'tute for what?"

"Nothing, dear. But just one thing, since you mention it. Or two, dear."

"Ugh."

"Did Helen know?"

"Helen who?"

"Armistead's Helen, silly."

"Oh, Miz Davis. She's always Miz Davis around here. Neva' Helen."

"Did she know?"

" 'Course, she knew. Whatta ya think she is? A moron? Darn right she knew. She's hated Carla's guts evah since." His voice started to trail away. "And Armistead's too, I think. That's one reason . . ."

"One reason for what?"

"Why Armistead left Virginia."

"Oh." Margaret thought for a long time. "Honey?"

"Ummmmm?"

"Honey, please."

"Umm?"

"What was the other reason?"

Raymond turned over, burrowing into the bedclothes, his breathing almost inaudible.

I guess I won't know the answer to that for some time, Margaret concluded. Then, again recalling Fogel Freiberg's confrontation with Armistead at dinner, she sat upright.

"Ray, are you still awake?"

"Oh God, Meg, what's it now?"

"Why did Armistead ask Freiberg about Mauve? Does he, I mean, did he, know her? She wasn't one of his . . . ?"

"Arm'stead knows evva'body."

"I keep thinking about her. I wonder why she wasn't at dinner. You don't think anything could have happened to her, do you?"

"Whatta ya mean, happen to her?"

"Oh, nothing, I guess. But I just keep thinking about her, that's all. Ray, are you still awake?"

"Ummmm . . ."

"Is it true what Fogel was saying about Mrs. Cosway? And, Ray, listen to me, honey, was Sally Hemings *really* Jefferson's wife's half-sister? I mean really? And who was their father? And Martha . . . My goodness. Ray?"

Her only reply was a placid snore, and before she had time to ponder further Margaret too was asleep.

CHAPTER 5

A MORNING DRIVE
IN ALBEMARLE COUNTY

Preach, my dear Sir, a crusade against ignorance; establish and improve the law for educating the common people. Thomas Jefferson to George Wythe, August 13, 1786

D RIVING INTO CHARLOTTESVILLE in the car provided them by the University, both Margaret and Raymond were in excellent spirits. Their slight hangovers had faded away during a breakfast of eggs and grits and fried apples and country sausage and coffee, and she looked, he had remarked, like a young girl. The morning air seemed to have been filtered through spring water and except for the phone call from Craig Babcock Raymond seemed at peace with the world.

"Dorsey's quite all right," the curator had said. "Nothing serious, just a very slight hairline fracture; she may be in a walking cast for a while, but otherwise she's fine. But could you all come out to the house as soon as possible? I need to talk with you before the others get here for lunch."

"Is it about Thorpe Taliaferro?" she had asked, after Craig, quite abruptly, had hung up. "And I'm glad that Dorsey's not seriously hurt."

"Partly about Thorpe." Raymond half closed his eyes and leaned toward her, simultaneously lowering his head and raising one arm. " 'J'accuse!' But mostly, I think, about Armistead and that crazy Freiberg." Freiberg with his wild statement about Maria Cosway, and Thorpe

mumbling in the men's room at Farmington after Craig
and Armistead had taken Dorsey Jack Morgan to the University hospital. "Believe me, Ray, the Great Man's a
thief. A thief," he'd repeated, but then Freiberg had
stepped from behind the door of one of the toilets. "I'll
discuss this with you tomorrow," Thorpe had said, his
eyes narrowing behind the Ben Franklins, and staggered
out of the men's room . . .

Now, stopping at the same intersection where yesterday
the Freibergs' spaniel had thrown up, Raymond pointed
toward the Old Gymnasium beyond the tennis courts
("That's where I used to fight"). The light turned and
they were driving past the Grounds (the chapel dun-colored in an abundance of pale spring greenery and darker
depths of carefully tended box); West Range ("Poe lived
there, and Woodrow Wilson"); the Rotunda with its tiers
of white marble steps descending to the larger-than-life
statue of The Founder on its massive pedestal ("There's
a better statue of Jefferson on the Lawn, you can't see it
from here"); the Serpentine Walls ("They were less expensive, that's why Jefferson designed them that way");
and the Long Walk to the Corner with its jumble of shops
on one side and the sprawling University medical center
on the other ("I wonder if Dorsey's still in there? She's
a lush, Meg, but you'll get to like her when you know her
better"). Down Main Street, past the deserted yards of
the Southern Railroad, the tracks rusted and refuse-dotted,
gritty grass sprouting dismally between the crumbling ties,
and beyond the tracks the depot, mass of weather-stained
brick and flaking dirty paint ("We always used to go there
after the fights; they used to have the best oysters in Char-

lottesville, everybody went there"). Another light, at the foot of Vinegar Hill where a waffle shop, gift house, service stations, and beauty school had replaced the pool parlors and run-down Negro restaurants ("Even on the coldest nights, everything was jumping and you could smell the frying fish; it was a good smell").

Beyond Vinegar Hill, Main Street formed a *V* around a deserted crumbling red-brick building. "That's the old high school, Meg, Lane High School," Ray said, and slowed the car as a small black child darted from the curb, almost plunging into the front fenders. He slammed on the brakes, and the engine coughed and stalled.

"Be careful," Raymond called, smiling, but the child did not return the smile; instead, he stuck out his tongue and made vaguely derisive wagging gestures with hands and shoulders before running across the street; at the same time, behind them a pale-faced pimply woman, hair in curlers, screeched the horn of her shabby sedan, which belched past them in a sooty flurry.

"The old order changeth, yielding place to new." She could not tell if Raymond heard her; he merely sighed deeply as they drove past another similarly deserted but tidier railroad depot, and over a bridge leading to a nondescript residential district with its scattering of shabby church, tacky filling station, junkyard, and auto graveyard.

"Pretend you don't see that," he said to Margaret, and then the city was fading behind them, the road became a divided highway, and the land suddenly, like a flower, opened up. Scrub land, pitted with outcroppings of limestone, was replaced by valley, gentle pastureland, and wooded hills, the dogwood not yet in open blossom, the redbud splashes of color against a backdrop of dark hickory and walnut. Now they were off the highway and ascending a narrow road which turned and twisted through tall stands of hickory and pine.

"That child." Raymond's tone was elegiac. "And that bitch in the purple car. You're right about the old order, Meg."

Behind them another horn honked briskly and a primrose sports car, top down, flashed past them. Raymond halted in the act of lifting an admonitory finger; the driver, who waved at them in friendly fashion before the car disappeared around a sharp curve, was Fogel Freiberg.

"Can you beat that? That madman!"

"He's something else, I'll say that."

"I wonder what he's up to this early in the morning." Raymond wiped his eyes. "I hope that joker's slowed down. He's going much too fast for this road."

"Was there a road in Jefferson's . . . sorry, *Mr.* Jefferson's time?"

"Sure, but ask Craig, he knows all the answers to that sort of thing. You know, almost until he died, it's said, Jefferson used to ride his horse down here and through Charlottesville to see how the work on the University was going. And he used to watch it through his telescope . . . imagine, he was in his eighties."

"Incredible!" Margaret took a deep breath. "How wonderful it must have been *then* . . . when Jefferson was alive. My goodness, look ahead!"

Fogel Freiberg, camera and folded tripod case at his

feet, stood in a hollow between road and forsythia-dotted slope; beside him lay the primrose MG, ditched. As they approached, the poet raised his arm and his grim face relaxed into a smile of recognition.

"Am I glad to see you already!" He chucked his thumb toward the MG. "Silly little car. Can't hold the road."

"Are you all right? Are you hurt?"

Grimacing slightly, he extended a bruised hand toward Margaret. "Only this." A smile flickered across Freiberg's face. "Fortunately, I wasn't driving fast."

"Of course." Raymond's voice was without humor. "We noticed that when you passed us."

"Here, let me take a look." Margaret reached for the swollen hand and the little man grimaced. "No, there doesn't seem to be any injury."

"Are you sure? Look, I can hardly move my fingers. They may be . . ."

"I think the car's in worse shape than your hand." Raymond pointed to the dark liquids, drop by slow drop, leaking from the underbelly of the MG.

"You win a few, Green, you lose a few. About the car, who cares?" Freiberg pointed to the handsome leather cases at his feet. "The cameras, they're O.K. I need to take pictures of Monticello — a lot of pictures, for my story. Without the cameras" — again he shrugged — "without them I'm helpless. Can you give me a lift?"

Raymond gestured vaguely. "We'll drop you off at the Tavern. There's a phone there; you can call Charlottesville for a towtruck or a wrecker." He turned away brusquely, too brusquely it seemed to Margaret, and took

a step toward their car, then hesitated momentarily before returning to the poet. "I'm glad the cameras weren't
hurt. Here, let me give you a hand with them."

The Tavern, Freiberg told Margaret as they slowly ascended the mountain after a moment or two of slightly
uncomfortable silence — Raymond had had his customary
difficulty starting the car — was a well-known inn during
the eighteenth century; Patrick Henry had lived in it, it
was his boyhood home; Monroe had stayed there occasionally during his presidency, had in fact entertained
Lafayette there; Jefferson had thought highly of it . . .

"You've done your homework, Freiberg, I'll say that. Or
did one of the girls in the office dig that up for you, like
that Maria Cosway story? I'd really like to hear more
about that sometime. You don't expect me to believe
that, do you?"

"As a matter of fact, Green, I *have* done my homework.
As for Cosway, you'd *better* believe it, but for now that's
classified. And Henry, I admire him."

"I never did think too much of him myself."

"Why not?"

Raymond made vague sweeping gestures with both
hands and the car swerved toward a tree-lined ravine.
"Henry really wasn't very much. A kind of ward politician."

"So what?" The poet's eyebrows rose dramatically.
"So what politicians aren't? What about Jefferson in the
campaign of eighteen-o-one? An idealist, you think? And,
Green, if you don't mind, will you watch where you're going, and keep your hands on the steering wheel?"

"It's the campaign of eighteen hundred, Fogel." Raymond's voice was as determined as Freiberg's eyebrows, but he returned his hands to the wheel. "And of course Henry did do some important things. But after the 'give me liberty or give me death' bit, his career — "

"Oh, Raymond!" From the corner of her eye Margaret glimpsed a gatehouse, split-rail fence, steeply rising pine-dotted lawn, and an imposing double-galleried house with several massive brick chimneys, all partially obscured by Fogel's dark curls. "I'm afraid we've passed it."

"Passed it? Passed what?"

"I'm not sure, but I think I just saw a sign, Mitchee Tavern."

"Mickey. M-i-c-h-i-e, but pronounced Mickey." Raymond glanced quickly at the rearview mirror, and again the car lurched toward the opposite side of the road. "You're right, Meg, we did pass it." He jerked the car to a swift halt and zigzagged back to the clearing in the pines. "Sorry, honey. Sorry, Freiberg. But you're essentially wrong about Patrick Henry. He's no hero, you know."

"Look, Green, I never said he was." Freiberg's pale face had taken on a slightly greenish hue, and beads of sweat dotted his creased forehead. "He's a man, but superman he's not. Like Jefferson, he's a man, that's all."

Surprising even Margaret, Raymond chuckled softly. "I'll go along with that." He backed the car clumsily off the road and onto a graveled driveway.

Once out of the car, Fogel Freiberg removed his wide-lapeled jacket and patted his forehead with the back of a heavily haired hand; his paisley neckerchief dangled askew over one shoulder and half-moons of sweat darkened the underarms of his lemon flannel shirt.

"Thanks very much for the lift." His lips were pale. "I'm glad I paid up my life insurance before I left New York. If you" — his dark eyes lingered on Margaret's face — "if you young people want to kill yourselves, that's strictly O.K. For myself" — he raised one shoulder — "I'm getting along in years, I've lived my life . . . Death in an automobile, it's no worse than cancer or emphysema."

He walked unsteadily up the curving brick walk to the long, low split-log building that formed an *L* with the many-galleried house. Beneath a sign, *The Ordinary,* the poet turned and faced them.

"I hope they serve drinks here." He ran his fingers through his disordered curls. "Care to join me?"

Raymond hesitated before slowly shaking his head. "I wish we could, but we've got to . . . we've got to move along." He gestured upward. "But thanks very much. We'll see you later." He started to turn the key in the ignition switch, but stopped and leaned from the window. "And, uh, Fogel, if you have any trouble getting the car fixed, get someone to call me. At Monticello. I'll come pick you up if you can't get a ride."

Once again on the road, he began to chuckle. "I wish we could have had a drink with him. You know, I'm beginning to like that little guy. In spite of myself, I'm beginning to like him."

CHAPTER 6

A CONFERENCE AT MONTICELLO WITH THE CURATOR

Never suppose, that in any possible situation, or under any circumstances, it is best for you to do a dishonorable thing, however slightly so it may appear to you. Whenever you are to do a thing, though it can never be known but to yourself, ask yourself how you would act were all the world looking at you. Thomas Jefferson to Peter Carr, August 19, 1785

R AYMOND HESITATED halfway up the broad brick walkway to the four-columned East Portico of Mr. Jefferson's house; as always he experienced the momentary shortness of breath that in his student years had accompanied his climbing into the ring before a boxing match.

. . . .

Domed and galleried the building rested like a red and white jewel on the very top of the green mountain so spacious so harmonious pillars and chimneys galleries and pavilions even the incongruously large weather vane at that very moment trembling in the soft midmorning breeze all blending into an ultimate oneness a total fusion of earth building and sky there are no things perfect in art he had written tritely but truly in the preface to his first book but there are those rare occasions when the creator can approximate the perfection inherent within a particular form in music the sixth Mozart viola quintet or the last of the piano concertos in sculpture the David *of Michelangelo or the Medici Venus in architecture Monticello Jefferson's own dear Monticello.*

. . .

He took a deep breath and started to speak but instead merely turned to Margaret, making a helpless rotating gesture with his shoulders. They walked slowly up the brick steps to the tall fanlighted door; then the door was opening; a middle-aged lady with a pleasant face and graying hair extended her hand to Margaret and smilingly inclined her head toward Raymond.

"Do come in, Mr. Babcock's expecting you. I'm Mrs. Pennyfeather, his hostess. He's been detained; he'll be down in a few minutes."

From polished hardwood floor to ivory-white ceiling, the room into which Mrs. Pennyfeather led them seemed to Margaret more like a museum than what one of Mr. Jefferson's grandchildren had once called the "most beautiful room I ever was in." Momentarily dwarfed by the high high walls, she was simultaneously overwhelmed and delighted. Recollections of her visit here with the Girl Scouts, memories from the picture books and history texts of her childhood, came suddenly, vividly, to life, heightened by the revelations of the previous night, to say nothing of the reading program she had embarked upon following Raymond's invitation to Virginia for Founder's Day. The pedestaled busts of Voltaire and Hamilton and Jefferson himself, and Turgot — whoever he was; the brass chandelier suspended from the center of the design of star-encircled eagle that dominated the ceiling; Jefferson bought that lamp in Paris, Ray was saying, his voice sounding faraway and remote. Could Maria Cosway have accompanied him on that long-gone shopping expedition? In Paris, she had read, people stopped and stared when

Jefferson — he was six feet four, sinewy, with a striking head and the palest blue-gray-green eyes; and he dressed in the height of fashion, knee breeches, silk stockings, embroidered waistcoats, the finest of lace ruffles — left his elegant house on the corner of the Grand Route of the Champs-Elysées and the rue Neuve de Berry, a house designed by the king's own architect, with magnificent gardens and courts, stables and carriage house. What a pair they must have made, the American minister plenipotentiary and his Maria, tiny, exquisite, animated . . .

Her eyes traveled from the ceiling to the entrance door and Mr. Jefferson's famous calendar clock with its weights of Revolutionary cannonballs: could it be true that Maria Cosway, hooded and furred, breathless with anticipation after a secret snowy carriage ride up Mr. Jefferson's beloved mountain, was it possible that she had stood beneath the clock that was ticking away at this very moment, waiting, breathless with anticipation and delight . . . ?

It is *not* possible, Raymond had stated at breakfast. Not possible, I don't believe it . . .

"Come out of it, honey; what're you thinking about?"

Margaret turned, smiling. Outside, on the porticoed porch, a group of tourists had assembled.

"This is the last group" — Mrs. Pennyfeather's voice was mildly apologetic — "to go through this morning; the house will be closed till two for the luncheon."

"There's something I want you to see before they come in," Raymond said in a low voice after the hostess had excused herself. He steered her toward the open French doors which led to the dining room at the opposite end of the hall, and stopped at a slender-legged mahogany table. Over the table, above a bowl of fresh daffodils, hung the portrait of a woman seemingly in her late fifties or early sixties, a woman wearing a beribboned hat tied in a loose bow beneath a strong but decidedly feminine chin, a woman with a handsome and slightly mocking face whose enigmatic blue-gray eyes seemed to contemplate the more familiar portrait on the opposite wall.

"So that's Martha! What a face! The mouth is Jefferson's, of course. You can recognize *that* immediately, Ray, and the forehead is too, as much as you can see of it beneath that cap. But her eyes, they're the saddest I've ever seen . . . they're almost Mona Lisa-ish."

"You can say that again." Raymond studied the portrait intently. "She earned those eyes, the hard way all right. Randolph was a wild man . . ."

"What's all this? What's all this about a wild man?" They turned quickly to confront the huge figure of Craig Babcock; beneath his smile the curator's face was lined with sleeplessness and worry.

"It was good of you all to come out: we've got lots of things to talk about. Classified, Meg, if you don't mind." He pulled a heavy gold watch from his pocket, glanced at it hastily, and grimaced. "Lord, they'll be getting here in an hour. Do you mind, Meg? If Ray and I go upstairs where we can talk? Mrs. Pennyfeather will show you around the house and the grounds."

"Of course, Craig. I've got lots of things I want to do. I want to see the Honeymoon Cottage — excuse me, the South Pavilion — and Colonel Randolph's Study and . . ."

Craig grinned. "You're a good woman, Meg."

She smiled and walked to the opposite side of the hall where Mrs. Pennyfeather was waiting for her beside the Rembrandt Peale portrait of Jefferson.

. . .

"Am I glad to see you." The curator led Raymond through a doorway and down a long narrow hall. "What a day this's been already. One of the really hairy ones. Dropped my razor this morning, smashed it to pieces, bumped my head getting into the car, then remembered I'd left the keys in the coat I had on last night, bumped my head getting *out* of the car to get the keys, that sort of thing."

At the foot of a steep flight of gray-carpeted steps, Craig paused. "Careful you don't stumble. They're mighty steep; sure wish Jefferson hadn't been so stingy when he planned *these*." At the third landing he stopped again, one huge hand on the dark polished wood of the banister, and exhaled heavily. "This is how I keep in shape nowadays, Ray. Climbing this mountain a dozen times every morning and afternoon. Phew."

He squeezed his huge bulk aside, waved Raymond into the room at the head of the stairs, and pointed to a chair covered in thread-worn faded provincial tapestry — "Sit down, *viejo*" — before easing himself into the swivel chair behind a desk littered with pamphlets, books, faded photostats, manuscripts, and a small vase filled with brightly colored straw flowers. He mopped his forehead, again exhaled deeply, and pointed to the battered typewriter on a metal stand beside the desk.

"You remember that, don't you? Same typewriter I had

when we were in graduate school." Craig smiled and tapped the keys. "Isn't that a beautiful sound? One of the oldest typewriters in the world. It belonged to my father, remember?" Once more he tapped the keys. "His first typewriter. They don't make them like that anymore . . . But I know you know I didn't ask you out here to talk about Dad's old typewriter." He fumbled a pack of cigarettes from the litter and extended it toward Raymond.

"No, thanks." Raymond's headshake was emphatic. "I'm really trying to quit for good this time."

The curator made no comment but after a brief pause rose uneasily and walked to the room's only window, lowering his head carefully to avoid the slanting ceiling. "Thank the dear Lord, the weather's O.K." Gingerly avoiding the books and journals scattered over the uncarpeted floor, he returned to his desk and breathed a mountainous sigh of relief. "Means we can go ahead and have the drinks on the Terrace, after all. It makes the board members happy." He withdrew his enormous watch and studied it with affection. "One of the oldest watches in the world." He smiled and glanced at the typewriter. "Also Dad's first."

"Come on, Craig, what's bothering you? I know it was a wild night, what with Dorsey and . . ."

Craig Babcock's groan was massive. "Damn Dorsey anyhow. Why did she have to choose this weekend to walk around the edge of the pool? Some damned reporter from the *Progress* just called me about that."

"Oh, it's not that bad; don't get so uptight about it."

"Not bad!" The curator swung around in his chair and waved his arms in a gesture that included his study, the house, the grounds, Charlottesville, Albemarle County, and the Commonwealth of Virginia itself. He stared at the framed drawings, engravings, and photographs on the walls between the crowded ceiling-high bookcases, all depicting Monticello — from Jefferson's own rough sketches and architectural drawings to some very recent color photographs by a distinguished French artist. "Not bad! Cock Almighty, Ray, what got into everybody last night? A witches' sabbath, if you ask me. Thorpe off his rocker!" Craig smiled at the recollection. "And that little smart-ass Freiberg . . . You don't believe all that hogwash he was dishing out, do you?"

"Can't really say. He sure bowled me over with that Maria Cosway business. I doubt the hell out of *that*." Raymond closed his eyes and gently stroked the flattened bridge of his nose. "But Jeff Randolph *did* withhold a lot of Jefferson papers that he thought were — what was his phrase? — 'not quite suitable for public scrutiny' or something of that sort. Like the Cosway-Jefferson letters; there's a lot of stuff — you know more about this sort of thing than I do — that's been stashed away, hidden for years, and finally turns up, like those books of Madison's you found at the University a couple of years ago. As for Martha and Jefferson . . ." Slowly Raymond stretched his legs as though to ward off a cramp. "Well, hell, Craig, you know that wasn't the customary father-daughter relationship, to put it mildly."

"Yeah, I guess you're right. You know, Ray" — the curator's voice was profoundly gloomy — "sometimes I wish I'd never taken this job." He exhaled heavily. "Cock Almighty!"

"Oh come on, Craig, you don't really mean that."

Monticello, he knew, had been Craig's life: he knew every nook and cranny of the house and the outbuildings, the details of kitchen and smokehouse, smithy and well and nailery; the history of everyone who had lived on the plantation; the depth of the fishpond and the species with which it was originally stocked; the variety of the flowers bordering the Roundabout Walk and the original trees of Mulberry Row . . .

"No, not really. But you ain't heard nothin' yet." Craig rose swiftly for a man of his size, almost knocking over the oldest typewriter in the world, and pointed to one of the pictures on the wall opposite Raymond. "Do you know what that is?"

Raymond took his glasses from his jacket pocket and carefully placed them over his broken nose before approaching the photograph of a blue-vaulted circular room with circular windows, a room empty except for a life-sized bronze statue of Jefferson in the center of the bare floor.

"Of course I know what it is." Raymond turned and pointed toward the ceiling. "It's the Dome Room, what Jefferson called the Sky Room. Armistead used to call it the Ballroom. You *know* I know what it is: remember the time he took us up there, when we were in graduate school, you and Dorsey and I . . . What is this, are you joking?"

"I wish I was." Craig pressed his finger tips against his temples. "I don't know where to begin, Ray . . . it's a long story." He drew in his breath like a diver about to take off from a high platform. "Somewhere up there, Ray, Armistead got hold of some papers."

"So that's what Thorpe was yakking about last night! I was — "

"Hold it down, Ray; just let me talk, will you?"

"O.K. O.K. Sorry, Craig."

"There're some bedrooms up there, you know: one of them's a double, it has two alcove bed recesses, the only double bedroom in the house . . ."

"Yeah, I know: they've imitated them at the Boar's Head."

"Please, Ray." Craig raised one large hand. "And the Randolphs lived up there, apparently — from time to time, that is."

"That's right, Craig. You know the letter, it's in the Trist Papers at the Library of Congress, isn't it? Martha wrote to Randolph when he was Governor, said she was getting one of the 'skylight' rooms ready for him."

"Damn it, Ray." The curator grinned. "Who's telling this story?"

"Sorry, Craig. Go on."

"It was late last fall, three or four months ago. We were having the Sky Room renovated, it'd been closed to the public for years, back before we were in school. It was in terrible shape; the floors were rotting, part of the ceiling and walls had fallen down . . . It'd been used as a storeroom, a junk room, you might say, for years . . . particularly after the War, after the overseer and his family'd moved in: chickens in the Entrance Hall, windows broken, bats in the Sky Room, that sort of thing." Craig shuddered and wrung his hands. "To this day it upsets me to think about it." He pulled out his watch and whistled involuntarily. "Ugh, it's getting near noon."

"Relax, Craig. Meg and Mrs. Pennyfeather — that's some name, incidentally; where'd you find *her?* — are down there. If Freiberg or anybody gets here early, they'll let you know."

"O.K. . . . As I said, we were having the place renovated. I had to go away for a couple of weeks, to some meetings or something. Workmen were all over the place, and Armistead was in and out all the time — he's always had the run of the house, you know. He must have gotten them then; they'd been plastered up behind the walls or beneath the old flooring or something . . ."

"Oh come on, Craig. That's hard to believe."

"I wish you were right, Ray. But it's true. I've suspected it for some time now, for the last few months, but I've never had the guts to come right out and speak to Armistead about it." Again Craig Babcock wrung his hands. "I've tried to a dozen times, but I just couldn't bring myself to do it. Lord, Ray, you know" — he hesitated — "you know how much I think of Armistead. He helped me get through graduate school, he got me this job." Craig shook his head slowly. "I'm not the best historian in the world, Ray, I know it as well as you do; Lord, man, I'd be teaching in some high school if it hadn't been for Armistead."

"Not true; cut that stuff out, Craig. But what *did* he find? And how'd you find out about it in the first place? How do you know . . . ?"

"One at a time, Ray. I don't know for sure . . . but it's pretty obvious they must have something to do with Patsy and the Colonel, and Sally Hemings, I expect; maybe even the Peter Carr business, and all that."

Raymond puffed out his cheeks and exhaled slowly. "By God, that would be something."

Again Craig looked at his watch. "You can say that again." He half rose from his chair but slumped back and looked squarely at Raymond. "I finally did speak to Armistead about it. Last night, after we'd taken Dorsey to the hospital . . . He was really smashed, sounded like he'd blown his mind. Said he was going to raise the roof in his lecture, 'Twilight at Monticello,' he's calling it; I'd never heard him talk like that before." Sighing, Craig withdrew a large handkerchief and mopped his forehead. "So, after we'd stashed Dorsey away for the night and were walking to the car, I finally did it, I asked him about the papers or whatever they were, where he'd gotten them, why he hadn't told me about it, everything." Again Craig mopped his forehead, shaking his head like a dog. "It wasn't easy, Ray."

"Lord no, I shouldn't think so. But what'd he say, how'd he react?"

"He said he'd tell me some other time, it was too important to talk about when he'd had that much to drink."

The phone on the desk buzzed and both men jumped.

"Just let it ring, I expect it's Mrs. Pennyfeather. I guess people are getting here."

At the door to the dimly lit hall he turned. "On top of everything else, Helen's on the warpath. All the women in her family have been slightly barmy, you know. She's fit to be tied 'cause Dorsey's here."

Raymond smiled. "I can't see why *that* would upset her."

"Very funny, Ray . . . And she's really furious about

Freiberg, too; did you see the way she was looking at him last night? Damn that little joker; that smart-ass business about Mrs. Jefferson and Sally Hemings really shook her up!"

"Well." Raymond's voice was apologetic. "I can't say I blame her, can you? After all, Helen *is* a descendant of Old Man Wayles."

"Trouble, trouble." Smiling ruefully, Craig paused at the head of the stairs. "Careful, Ray, these steps are dangerous . . . It was good of you to be my crying towel. We'll talk about all this later; till then keep it under your hat, huh?"

"Sure, Craig . . . and keep my eyes and ears open?"

"Yup, eyes and ears open."

Shaking his huge head and with one hand on the banister, the curator started down the stairs.

CHAPTER 7

SHERRY ON THE TERRACE

*And our own dear Monticello, where
has nature spread so rich a mantle under the eye? mountains, forests, rocks,
rivers. With what majesty do we there
ride above the storms!* Thomas Jefferson to Maria Cosway, October 12, 1786

I WONDER what can be keeping Ray, Margaret thought as she stood alone in the *L* formed by the South Terrace Walk and the Promenade leading to the conservatory of Mr. Jefferson's mansion. Shaking her head she looked at the backs of Webster and Carla Eppes as they walked stiffly toward the small group assembled on the Promenade: What a pair that is! Beneath her — she knew from her recent tour of the house and grounds with Mrs. Pennyfeather and from Craig Babcock's excellent book on the subject — were what Mr. Jefferson had called his "offices": dairy, servants' quarters, smokehouse, and kitchen, now restored but unused. Behind her, the South Walk terminated in a small gem of a red-brick pavilion to which Mr. Jefferson had brought his bride, Martha Wayles Skelton, one snowy January evening almost two hundred years ago. Opposite it, at the north end of the mansion, a similar walk terminated in a similar building, Colonel Randolph's Study or law office. What secrets, Margaret thought, *that* building might reveal.

Ahead and to her left was the graceful white-columned East Front; beyond it lay hill, pasture, valley, and beyond them the blue-gray mountains. To the north, above the still-bare hilltop trees, Margaret, standing for a moment on tiptoe, could catch a glimpse of Charlottesville and the University of Virginia.

It was a beautiful morning, as Mrs. Pennyfeather had recently reminded her, even for Virginia in mid-April. The scent of green growing things was in the air, mingling with the fragrance of dry sherry and the more assertive bouquet of excellent bourbon. Although the peaks of the distant Blue Ridge were capped with snow, the air felt warm and gentle.

I wonder what can be keeping Ray, Margaret thought, regarding Dorsey Jack Morgan, conspicuous in the midst of one of the small groups assembled on the Promenade. The archivist was dressed in a suit of the most exquisite pale gray flannel; even with one of her lovely legs in a cast she looked as fresh as the claret pansies and white hyacinths in the myrtle-edged beds along the brick walk that descended to the white Chinese trellis gates. Margaret started to wave to Miss Morgan but hesitated as the archivist leaned over to say something to Fogel Freiberg, who threw back his head and laughed convulsively. Momentarily embarrassed, Margaret tried unsuccessfully to beckon one of the white-jacketed waiters bearing silver trays dotted with glasses of sherry, but stopped as Raymond emerged from the French door next to the conservatory, scanned the crowd on the Promenade, and, finally seeing her, hastened toward her.

"Am I glad to see you! My goodness, Ray, what kept you so long?"

"Craig had to go back to get some papers he'd left upstairs, then Mrs. Pennyfeather had to see him about something, then the phone rang, all that sort of thing. Gosh,

Meg, I'm sorry. But how'd you and Mrs. Pennyfeather make out, huh?"

"Oh, I've got so much to tell you. I'm glad you're back, I hate being by myself at a time like this. She took me all over the place. That pavilion" — she turned and pointed behind her — "where Jefferson and his wife spent their honeymoon! It's really marvelous. Fireplace, a spinning wheel, candlesticks, and a beautiful Federal mirror. To say nothing of the chairs — you know, Mrs. Pennyfeather told me that some of the chairs were made by one of the slaves . . . guess who, Sally Hemings's brother. Can you imagine? And what a four-poster bed! You can really visualize what it must have been like that night when they arrived in the snowstorm. Delicious! And — "

"And Colonel Randolph's, uh, law office. Did she show you that?"

"You bet she did! It's delicious, too. More masculine, naturally; it even has a corner cupboard filled with law books. And did you know there's a stairway in one corner of the room? You can just see the beginning of a flight of stairs from where I was standing." Margaret paused and lowered her voice. "You must tell me more about Colonel Randolph. I asked Mrs. Pennyfeather about him and if she knew where the steps led to, but she seemed a little upset. Said she didn't know, and changed the subject." Margaret raised her eyebrows conspiratorially. "What do you think of that? Was she hiding something? Did Colonel Randolph have — have anything to do with Sally Hemings?"

"Take it easy, Sherlock; some of these rumors you've been hearing are beginning to get to you."

"You can say that again. I'm dying to talk with you alone." She looked around as though someone might be eavesdropping. "Mrs. Pennyfeather's something of a gossip. She told me, or rather sort of hinted, some very int'resting things. She's a kind of mother hen. She adores Craig, of course, but she's not too fond of Armistead. Or of Carla, either. And I can't say I blame her. About Carla, that is. That woman! I was standing there waiting for you, and Carla came up. Very busy, very officious. Just talked for a minute. Before Webster Eppes showed up." She imitated Carla's voice, the kind of voice Raymond had always associated with vice presidents of garden clubs or local historical societies. " 'Disgustin' behayvyuh of Mista' Tollivuh last night. Simply disgustin'. Mista' Eppes was outraged. Simply outraged!' She was really getting wound up, but then Webster came over and they left, just before you came out."

"Led her away screaming, eh? She's a case, all right; I'd hate to have her sink her fangs into me. Got a mind like a sewer, too, that baby. But what'd she say about Armistead? I've got something to tell you about him, incidentally."

"I thought that's what Craig wanted to talk about. Where is Armistead, by the way? And Helen?" Margaret scanned the crowd on the Promenade and again marveled at the sight of Dorsey Jack Morgan: at this distance the slight worry lines around the archivist's mouth and eyes were invisible and in the clear sunny air a halo seemed to be hovering above her ash-colored hair. "She's incredible, that woman."

She turned to Raymond, who in the act of beckoning

to one of the waiters had caught Miss Morgan's eye instead. Is there more to that exchange of glances, Margaret wondered, than simple recognition?

"Who? What do you mean, incredible?"

Arthur, the headwaiter, approached, smilingly extending a tray to Raymond, who removed two glasses of sherry; almost simultaneously Dorsey Jack Morgan hobbled over to them followed by Fogel Freiberg.

"Aren't we being exclusive this morning? Hello, Margaret, dear. Good morning, or rather good afternoon, Professor Green. My goodness, how well you both look! Margaret, your earrings are beautiful, simply beautiful." Bending over, she examined the jade circles.

"We're fine, thank you. And I'm glad you like the earrings. Ray bought them for me in Mexico." She glanced at Miss Morgan's sheath-encased leg. "And how are you?"

Dorsey Jack Morgan smiled in genuine self-deprecation. "Much better than I have any right to be. God takes care of fools, and all that sort of thing, you know."

"Good. And you, Fogel?" Raymond regarded with some envy the glass of bourbon and water in the poet's hand. "Did you get your car taken care of?"

"Actually no. Cheers. Miss Morgan is taking care of it for me."

"That's extremely decent of Miss Morgan."

Freiberg ignored Raymond's heavy-handed irony. "I couldden' get hold of the garage. So I was sitting by the road wondering what to do when fortunately who should drive by but Miss Morgan and" — he paused and jerked his thumb toward the group on the Promenade where Thorpe Taliaferro, spring flower in his tan-and-white hound's-tooth jacket, stood alone, nervously smoking and studying them covertly, twiddling his sherry glass while pretending to stare across the valley — "and What's-his-name. So I came up with them. And Miss Morgan, like I said, she's going to call someone to fix the car."

"How very nice for you."

Freiberg's reply was halted by the reappearance of Carla Eppes, who leaned toward him, drawn, as it were, by the weight of her great breasts. "Oh, Mista' Frayberg, ah heah you'v had trubble with yawr cyah. An' how is yawr waf' today? Ah do hope she's betta' an' can jawn us this evenin'. Mista' Eppes tells me youah goin' ta write the most preshus stawry faw yawr magazine. About *ouah* Monticella. Just let me know if theyah's ennathin' ah can do to assist ya? And ah do hope deah Miz Frayberg can jawn us. An' how is yawr deah little cockerel spanyel?"

Dorsey Jack Morgan regarded Carla, who had ignored all of them except Freiberg, with contempt. "What do you think" — her voice was very low — "what *do* you think of *our* Monticello, Margaret?"

"What can I say?" Margaret raised her hands helplessly. "It's so . . . forgive the triteness, Dorsey. It's simply wonderful."

"You *have* been here before, then, haven't you? In spite of what you said last night." Again the archivist glanced with open contempt at Carla, who had placed her hands gently on Freiberg's narrow shoulders and appeared to be in the process of embracing him with her breasts.

Margaret hesitated a moment before replying, smiling in spite of herself. "Yes, but it was a long time ago. When I was a Girl Scout. How did you know?"

"My radar, I guess." She gestured toward Raymond, who had been glancing from Margaret and Dorsey to Carla Eppes and Freiberg. "And when you said it there was a look on the face of one of my favorite Jefferson scholars . . ."

Margaret laughed; it was impossible for her not to like Miss Morgan. "One of your favorite Jefferson scholars is going to get into a peck of trouble if he isn't more careful."

"What's that? What's that about Jefferson scholars?"

"Nothing, dear."

"I was admiring Margaret's earrings, Ray; they're simply beautiful."

Lifting her chin as though to display the earrings, Margaret was suddenly conscious of the presence of Helen Davis a short distance from them, nose slightly raised as though, like Soames Forsyte, she was sniffing something unpleasant. Catching Margaret's eye, Mrs. Davis smiled coolly, and Margaret nodded in return while Dorsey Jack Morgan lifted one hand in a friendly gesture. As Carla Eppes continued to cuddle Freiberg, Thorpe Taliaferro hesitantly approached the group, bowing to Mrs. Davis in passing. However, she looked him straight in the eye without speaking; Taliaferro stroked his mustaches in embarrassment, started to return to his solitary post on the Promenade, then after a moment or two of indecision joined the group. One of the waiters approached and Taliaferro shook his head sadly at the sight of the sherry. Turning to Freiberg, who had freed himself from Carla Eppes, he suddenly realized that the poet was drinking whiskey.

"Where'd you get *that?* I haven't seen any of *that*

around." He leaned forward, spilling cigarette ashes into Freiberg's drink.

"Oh, didn't you know?" Dorsey Jack Morgan gestured toward the house. "It's in the tearoom."

"I wish I'd known that sooner." Taliaferro placed his sherry glass on the railing, and departed hastily.

"Mr. Jefferson didn't approve of 'spirits,' you know, Margaret. Never, or seldom ever, served them at Monticello. But Craig — "

Craig Babcock suddenly emerged from one of the clusters in the middle of the Promenade. "What's this? Is someone taking my name in vain?"

"I was just telling Margaret about the whiskey."

"Thanks, Dorsey." The curator turned to Raymond. "I meant to tell you there's bourbon inside if you want it. In the past we've had only sherry at these occasions. In deference to Jefferson. But our hard-drinking scholars complained, so this year we decided to serve drinks."

"I'll drink to that," laughed Fogel Freiberg as Thorpe Taliaferro reappeared smiling and carrying a glass of bourbon and water in each hand.

"So will I." Thorpe took a grateful swallow. "This is more like it. Ahhh. Much more like it." Trying unsuccessfully to catch Raymond's eye, he took another generous draft, as Craig Babcock, on the lookout for Armistead Davis and seeing Helen Davis standing alone, excused himself and hastened toward her.

"Won't you join us, Mrs. Davis?"

"Thank you, Craig, but if you don't mind I'll just wait here. For Armistead."

"Of course."

He bowed slightly, excused himself, and returned to the group.

"Where's Davis, Babcock? I'd like to ask him a question or two."

"He should be here any minute now, Fogel."

"I talked with him on the phone this morning." Dorsey Jack Morgan addressed Margaret rather than anyone else. "He called me about my leg."

"Ah yes, your leg, Miss Morgan." Fogel Freiberg studied the sheath thoughtfully. "I shall compose a poem to commemorate your injury."

"Oh, that would be wonderful."

Craig Babcock, apparently not enjoying such small talk, turned to Margaret. "You haven't seen all of the gardens yet, Meg; how about taking a walk around the Roundabout? Anybody else care to join us? Ray?"

"I sure would. Excuse us, Dorsey, will you?"

Raymond started to leave but Thorpe Taliaferro followed him, reaching out for his arm as they approached the steps leading from the Promenade.

"Wait a minute, old buddy. I want to talk with you. About Armistead."

"O.K., O.K. You all go on, Craig. I'll be with you in a minute."

He regarded Thorpe with some irritation; the librarian's eyes behind the Ben Franklins seemed simultaneously enlarged and dwarfed, and Raymond had the sensation of peering into two whirlpools, eddying in ever more rapid circles.

"I've been wanting to talk with you." Taliaferro's voice was intense and urgent; beneath the librarian's impeccable Saltz Brothers madras shirt Raymond could almost sense the rapid beating of his heart. "Will you stop fidgeting and listen to me, Ray? What I said last night isn't the half of it."

"Sure, Thorpe, I'd like to talk. But can't we get together after lunch?"

He started to follow Craig and Margaret but stopped at the sound of Armistead Davis's voice. Brandishing his cigarette holder, the biographer appeared at the head of the wooden steps from the offices below, followed by a small, almost completely bald man with a sunburned vaguely European face, thick-lensed glasses, and wearing an immaculate old-fashioned blue-and-white seersucker suit.

"Look, you all." Armistead's voice was as unsteady as his gait, his handsome face was flushed and beaded with perspiration. "Look who's here. Look who's come up from Westmoreland County!"

"Rod! Oh, but it's good to see you." Helen Davis ignored her husband and hugged the little man delightedly as Craig and Margaret returned from the entrance to the Roundabout to join the small group converging upon Armistead and the little man. For the first time, Margaret thought, Mrs. Davis seems to have come alive.

"This is just wonderful!" Helen Davis exclaimed.

A sunburned man with the genial, slightly bemused expression of an elderly country doctor or a retired small-town lawyer, John Rodney had survived them all, all his friends and fellow writers of the great years — Sherwood Anderson, F. Scott Fitzgerald, Ernest Hemingway, William Faulkner, and all the rest. Now in the twilight of his distinguished career, he divided his time between his Virginia home and Baltimore, living quietly but still writing despite the automobile accident which years before had taken the life of his young wife and the sight of one of his eyes.

"Helen." He pressed his cheek against hers. "Ah, Helen, you're beautiful!"

"What a surprise!" She glanced coolly at Armistead. "*He* hadn't told me."

"I really wasn't planning to come. I have to go to Hopkins next week for my annual checkup, and I've been taking it easy. But when Arm'stead called me last night and said he was going to make a speech" — John Rodney gestured with Latin enthusiasm — "I simply couldn't resist."

"I'll tear their hearts out, now that you're here. By God, I will."

Ignoring Armistead's comment, Helen Davis turned to John Rodney and again kissed him on the cheek. "Oh, you look *so* good. How *are* you, Rod?"

"I feel fine, the farm air does things for me, you know. And Monticello always makes me feel good." Waving his hands as though to embrace Mr. Jefferson's plantation, he saw Raymond, who had rejoined Margaret. "Is that Raymond Green over there? What are you hiding back there for, Ray?" Advancing nimbly, both arms outstretched, he placed a freckled hand on Raymond's shoulder. "Arm'stead told me you were going to be here. And married, too. This must be Margaret." He took her hand gently and raised it to his lips, smiling warmly before returning to Raymond. "Congratulations; you're a lucky man."

"We're all lucky now that you're here." Beaming, Craig Babcock waved his arms enthusiastically. "It'll be a great day. It's been too long since you did any work here."

"Oh, I don't write much anymore." John Rodney smiled apologetically. "That last book on Jefferson just about did me in, you know; it's about time I left that sort of thing to Arm'stead and the young fellows like Ray. And I've got to get back to the farm tomorrow; one of the mares is about to drop a foal." He paused for breath, peering upward, as though searching the sky for signs of rain. "But I did want to see you all, and hear Arm'stead. He's going to rattle a few skeletons tonight, he tells me. Aren't you, Arm'stead?"

Was she imagining or did Margaret hear an almost inaudible but immediately identifiable gagging sound behind her from Webster Eppes, who had quietly slithered his way toward the group on the Terrace.

"You can say that again, Rod." Armistead pointed toward the brick pavilion at the end of the North Terrace Walk. "Heads will roll tonight, that's for sure." At the sudden concern on Craig Babcock's face, he stopped and carefully inserted a fresh cigarette in his black holder. "Don't let Rod upset you, Craig; it won't be as dramatic as he suggests." After lighting the cigarette, his hand shaking ever so slightly, he squinted in the direction of Colonel Randolph's Study. "But let's drink to Rod and to Mr. Jefferson." A satyrlike smile flickered across his lips. "And to the ladies, of course, all the dear dead ladies."

Craig beckoned to Arthur, who soon returned with a tray, glasses of sherry, a silver ice bucket, and a king-sized decanter of whiskey. There was much talk and laughter and then a moment of silence broken by Armistead's slurred voice.

"Relax, Craig; don't worry."

"Of course not, Craig." Webster Eppes's lips were smiling but beneath his dryly cultivated voice was an undercurrent of venom. "You don't have to worry about anything Armistead might say."

"Well, now." Armistead ran his hand through his thick white hair, and swayed ever so slightly, regarding Webster with only the shadow of a patronizing smile. "Of course . . ." He paused to glance again at the small pavilion and then down toward the unseen servants' quarters. "Of course, I could change my mind. I could talk about the Colonel's pecca — peccadillas. Or about Martha Jefferson." He drained his drink. "Or even about Black Sally."

"Arm'stead always makes a good speech." Carla Eppes smiled enigmatically. "No matter what he's talkin' about."

Armistead bowed from the waist, almost but not quite in a parody of eighteenth-century courtliness. "Thank you, my dear. That's very gen'rous of you."

Carla Eppes's hand tightened around her glass, a flicker crossed her chipmunk face, and her voluptuous bosom seemed to swell like a pigeon's. God in Heaven, Raymond thought, suddenly breaking into a sweat, she's going to toss that glass at Armistead. But the tension-filled moment passed as Carla's pink and white mask relaxed.

"Thank *you,* Arm'stead."

Mrs. Pennyfeather appeared at the far end of the Promenade, caught Craig Babcock's eye, and nodded.

"Time for lunch, you all." The curator's voice was warm with relief. "Shall we, uh, go inside?"

CHAPTER 8

DESCENT FROM THE MOUNTAINTOP

I now see our fireside formed into a group, no member of which has a fibre in their composition which can ever produce any jarring or jealousies among us. Thomas Jefferson to Martha Jefferson Randolph, June 8 1797

BEHIND THE HIGH BLACK IRON FENCE the obelisk marking Mr. Jefferson's resting place dwarfed the headstones and tablets warmed by the midafternoon sun which cast flickering arabesques at the foot of the tall pine behind the obelisk: except for the fence, Margaret thought, the burying grounds at Monticello seemed more like a garden than a place of death, evoking in her the same feeling of harmony and repose as the building they had just left. She tried the handle of the arched and scrolled gateway, surprised at its resisting coldness, and in disappointment turned to Raymond and Thorpe Taliaferro, who had paused at the foot of the brick steps leading to the graveyard.

"It's locked, Ray. I wish we could go inside and look around."

"It's always locked, but we can get in tomorrow; there'll be a memorial service here then. I think you'd like it. How about you, Thorpe, care to join us?"

"At a *religious* ceremony?" The librarian's voice was incredulous. "Certainly not! Surely you don't think that Jefferson would approve of *that* sort of thing, do you?"

"Oh, come on, Thorpe, it's not that bad. It's really quite nice, Meg; I've been to a couple of them." Raymond pointed beyond the gate. "A lot of the Jefferson descendants are buried there, too. Usually some of *their* descendants — small children, mostly — lay wreaths on the grave, and there's taps and a prayer, very brief, that sort of thing." He paused, searching for words. "It's quite, uh, impressive."

"Yukkkhh! Last year a squad of jokers from the Charlottesville National Guard — in costume, no less, I wouldn't call them uniforms — fired a six-gun salute. If that's what you call impressive, Ray, you can have it. And there were a lot of old ladies from the Monticello Family Association and the Colonial Dames and the U.D.C., all simply slobbering to get into the act." Thorpe Taliaferro's pale hands fluttered like moths. "Even President Nixon sent a wreath. You can have it, Ray, just don't try to sell it to me."

What a really strange man he is, Margaret thought; so predictably unpredictable. Seated next to her at lunch he had chatted engagingly — it was the first time she really had been able to understand his slow, slurred speech — about nothing in particular, completely ignoring the other guests at their table; then as they were leaving the dining room he had beckoned to Raymond and in a low conspiratorial voice had asked for a ride with them back to the Boar's Head. Of course, Raymond had said, after a momentary hesitation, making a definite effort to control his irritation . . .

"I'm not trying to sell you a damned thing, Thorpe; I couldn't care less. I think we'll come out for it, don't you, Meg?"

Before she could reply he took her hand and they peered

through the spokes of the fence. " 'It covers the grave of Jefferson,' " he read slowly from the inscription at the base of the obelisk, " 'his wife, his two daughters, and of Governor Thomas Mann Randolph, his son-in-law.' "

In some surprise Ray turned to Thorpe Taliaferro, the irritation drained from his voice.

"You know, I'd forgotten that. I didn't remember that the Colonel was buried there too. All of them together, finally: Jefferson, his wife, the two daughters, *and* Randolph."

"That's about the only time they *were* together. What a ménage!" Twirling his mustaches, Thorpe glared myopically at Raymond. "Why not Sally Hemings, too? She has as much right to be in there as Colonel Randolph. Or Mrs. Cosway, for that matter, if what that ass Freiberg was saying's true." He turned almost angrily to Margaret, his mustaches bristling. "Colonel Randolph was a very sick man, Mrs. Green. An alcoholic *and* a lecher . . . and he hated Jefferson's guts."

"Oh come *on,* Thorpe; Randolph was peculiar but — "

"Peculiar! You call poker-whipping his son-in-law *peculiar?* You call riding that damned horse of his — what was its name . . . Dromedary? — across the fields knocking hell out of the sheaves the slaves had been working on all day — just because he wasn't satisfied with the job — you call that just *peculiar?* And not coming to see Jefferson when the old man was dying . . . not even going to the funeral, but hiding out up there on the mountain in his study — 'Colonel Randolph's law office!' Ugh! Law office, my ass, he probably used that just for sleeping off hangovers or shacking up with one of the slaves. Do you call

all that *peculiar?* And all those children." The librarian
glared at Margaret, his face taut. "Faugh! How many
were there? A dozen! A regular breeding machine, that's
what he was. No wonder Martha ran away! No wonder
she wanted to be with Jefferson! And those names! James
Madison Randolph! Patrick Henry Randolph! George
Wythe Randolph! Why not Jesus H. Christ Randolph!
You call that just *peculiar?* Bah!"

Smiling in spite of himself, Raymond turned to Margaret. "Randolph *was* a nut in a lot of ways, Meg, you've
heard me say that before. But he was a great man, too.
Now just wait a minute, will you?" He held up an admonishing hand as the librarian opened his mouth and leaned
forward to interrupt. "You're quite wrong about his hat-
ing Jefferson; you're ignoring the basic facts and empha-
sizing a few, uh, incidents late in Jefferson's life. And as
for the kids — and there were eleven, Thorpe, not twelve
— well, every man to his own taste and all that, but that
doesn't make him a lecher. So he *was* an alcoholic, there's
ample proof of that, and a real oddball, but don't give me
that old poontang routine . . ."

"What are you, a Pollyanna or something?" Taliaferro
grinned wolfishly, raised one long arm and pointed a
skinny finger at Raymond. "You know all that business involving Randolph and . . ."

"Look, Thorpe." Raymond sat down grumpily, Margaret beside him, and gazed into the quiet graveyard.
"Don't blame Jefferson for anything Colonel Randolph
might have done. Or might *not* have done, for that matter. First of all, I *don't* know what you mean by 'all that
business involving Randolph.' Don't call me a Pollyanna;

if anything irritates me, it's for someone to call me a Pollyanna. Randolph had nothing to do with Sally Hemings and neither did Jefferson; I'm fed up to to here with all that. And don't give me that incest routine, either. If that's what you've been wanting to talk to me about, skip it."

Shaking his shoulders irritably, Raymond reached for Margaret's hand and half rose to his feet.

"Now wait a minute, old buddy." At the gentleness of the librarian's voice Raymond regarded him quizzically for a long moment and then, grumbling, sat down. "I've had a bellyful of that, too. I guess." He turned to Margaret. "I imagine Ray's told you all that crap about Jefferson being a racist, and Sally Hemings being the mother of his bastards and . . ."

"Knock it off, Thorpe, Sally wasn't Jefferson's, uh, mistress. O.K., so there were a lot of mulattoes up there" — and Raymond gestured toward the house at the top of the hill — "but they weren't Jefferson's. They were probably Peter Carr's."

"O.K., O.K." Again Thorpe Taliaferro's pale hands fluttered above his oblong head. "If you'll just let me speak, Ray. I never said they were Jefferson's." He made a sour face. "You see, Mrs. Green, I don't believe all that — if you'll excuse my language — that bullshit. It's Armistead not me" — his voice rose — "who's so big on it; just wait" — and he glared through his heavy Ben Franklins at Raymond — "till you hear the Old Stud's talk tonight."

"How do you know what Armistead's going to talk about tonight? Who do you think you are anyway, Jesus

Christ? You got a hot line to Armistead's mind? What've you got against Armistead anyhow?"

"Now, Ray." Margaret placed a hand on Raymond's knee and looked with some trepidation at the tall figure of Thorpe Taliaferro, his arms waving like an Old Testament prophet's.

"I've got *plenty* against Armistead. That's what I've been wanting to talk with you about, Ray. You must know by now about the stuff he stole from the Dome Room and's planning to peddle on Madison Avenue. If you haven't, you're about the only one who hasn't." He hesitated, a slight smile creasing his pale cheeks. "There's still an honor system at the University, isn't there? What'll they do? Kick the Old Stud out when they hear about it? The Great Man's a thief, Ray, so don't give *me* any of that Jesus Christ stuff. You're the one who's always talking about Jefferson like that."

Raymond, after a moment of uncertain silence, began to smile. He stretched out, thoughtfully massaging the calf of one of his legs, glanced at the obelisk beyond the iron fence, and smiled again. Warm rays of the afternoon sun slanted through the tall trees of the burying grounds, the brick steps against their bottoms were surprisingly comfortable; all the tension had vanished and Raymond was chuckling quietly and gazing again at the obelisk.

"Whatever are you laughing at, dear?"

Raymond pointed to the obelisk. "That. That and what Thorpe just said. They reminded me of a story. Suddenly I remembered a story. One that Armistead told me. I hadn't thought of it for years. I expect you've heard it, Thorpe, it's an old Mafia story, but I know Meg hasn't."

Raymond rubbed his forehead with his finger tips. "Let's see, how does it begin? Ahhh, yes. Armistead and Mrs. Davis were living in Cambridge; it was just after he'd left Virginia to take a professorship at Harvard. One of his nephews was living with them, he was just a child, four or five years old, something like that. I think he was the son of one of Armistead's sisters; I don't really remember, but that's not important. Growing up in that household, he heard a lot about Jefferson, like from morning till night; he probably knew more about Jefferson than most historians. Right, Thorpe?"

The librarian did not answer but nodded slightly.

"Well, the boy had never been to Monticello, so one time when Armistead had to come to Charlottesville to do some research, they brought him with them and one of the first things he wanted to do was to go to Monticello."

"Sounds improbable. I expect it was the Old Stud who wanted to drag the brat along."

Raymond grimaced, but regarded the librarian tolerantly.

"O.K., Thorpe, maybe you're right. But that's the way Armistead told it . . . So he took the boy through the house, and on the way back they stopped here at the graveyard. They went inside. Apparently the place wasn't locked up then the way it is now, Meg. The boy stood there a long time, staring at the Jefferson tombstone, but not saying anything. Just stood there and stared. Finally he took a backward step. He seemed puzzled, extremely puzzled. He looked to the right of the monument and then to the left. Seemed even more puzzled than before, but didn't say a word. Just looked again to the right and then to the left. Finally he turned to Armistead, more bewildered than ever."

Raymond paused and looked at Margaret expectantly.

"And?" she asked. "What happened then? What did the boy say?"

Raymond hesitated, smiling broadly in anticipation. " 'But Uncle Armistead,' he asked. 'Where are the graves of the two thieves?' "

Ignoring a slight groan from Thorpe, Raymond slapped his thigh appreciatively and rose, chuckling. "Let's get going, shall we?" He squinted at the sun. "It's getting late."

"That's a good story, Ray." Margaret extended her hand and Raymond pulled her to her feet. She began to laugh, as much at the story as at Thorpe who stood beside them, stroking his mustaches with long fingers and regarding them speculatively. Then, silently, they descended the brick steps and started to their car. Halfway across the narrow road, Taliaferro turned and squinted at them through his glasses.

"You're right, Mrs. Green. It *is* a good story . . ."

"Watch out, Thorpe, for God's sake!"

Raymond pushed Margaret back, seized the librarian's arm and jerked him aside as a car swept around the curve in the road a few yards from them, a pale blue Volvo driven much too rapidly by Fogel Freiberg, accompanied by a smiling Dorsey Jack Morgan who waved at them enthusiastically and called out "Helloyouallseeyoulaytuh . . ."

"Jesus!" Thorpe exhaled slowly and crossed the road, shaking his head and muttering in disbelief. He leaned against the hood of Raymond's car and with trembling hands withdrew a leather-covered flask from the depths of his tweed jacket. He carefully unscrewed the shiny metal covering cap, fumbled momentarily with the plastic screw-on top beneath it, and glanced at Margaret apologetically before lifting the flask in a half salute.

"I'm sorry I can't offer you a drink, Mrs. Green."

"Of course. Thanks very much anyhow and, please, Thorpe, it's Margaret."

He smiled and took a grateful swallow. "Thanks, Margaret. Thank you very much. And you too, Raymond; you damn near saved my life." He gestured toward the road and again drank from the flask. "Had I known we were likely to be . . . murdered by maniacs I'd have brought along a half gallon and a jug of spring water." He took a final swallow, his Adam's apple bobbing in the process, and patted his lips with a linen handkerchief before squinting into the flask. Sadly he shook his head and turned it upside down; one last golden drop formed slowly at the lip and splattered into the dust.

"All good things must come to an end, I guess." Smiling ruefully, he returned the flask to his pocket. "Tell you what, let's stop at Michie's on the way down. I'd like to buy you all a drink."

. . .

"You know, I did an article about that tombstone a few years ago," Raymond volunteered as they slowly drove down the winding road. "The original obelisk was chipped to pieces by souvenir hunters and eventually had to be replaced. There was legislation about it in Congress — this was in the late eighteen seventies as I recall — and a lot of hubbub about the disposition of the obelisk. Some of the administrators from Missouri — the dean of the university and the president, both, were Virginians; one of them had, as a matter of fact, served with Lee from the beginnings all the way to Appomattox, and after all Missouri was the first state university in the Louisiana Purchase territory and . . ."

"Don't forget to stop at Michie's." Thorpe Taliaferro's voice was urgent. "It's just around the next bend."

"Sure, sure, I could use a drink myself. And, well, the University of Missouri eventually got the tombstone. I did a little article about it a few — "

"Oh dear, Raymond, you're passing it again!" Raymond made a desperate U-turn and in a flurry of gravel pulled into the parking lot, where he surveyed the scene with quiet satisfaction.

As he gingerly stepped from the back seat, Thorpe Taliaferro smiled faintly; momentarily buoyed up by his drinks, he seemed more cheerful than at any time since their meeting at the Falstaff Room.

"I'd like to see a copy of that article some time, Ray; it sounds int'restin'. But first things first, you know." Thorpe nodded expectantly toward the Ordinary. "Business before pleasure and all that sort of thing." He strode ahead briskly, but halted as though a coiled snake had suddenly materialized at his feet. At the far end of the parking area was the pale blue Volvo.

"Well, what do you know?" Thorpe Taliaferro shook his head and glanced suspiciously around the lot before removing his glasses and scrutinizing the thick lenses as though they held the clue to a riddle. Again he shook his head, and stroked his mustaches with one bony hand. "Our good friends" — his voice trembled slightly as he replaced his glasses and turned to Raymond and Margaret, who hesitated behind him — "our good friends have apparently entertained the same idea. I'm . . . delighted. You know, Mrs. Green . . . Margaret . . . for many generations Jeffersonians and non-Jeffersonians alike have paused here to . . . to refresh themselves." He squared his angular shoulders and walked resolutely to the door of the Ordinary, pausing to admire the huge black iron bell flanked by sheaves of varicolored Indian corn and a massive stone crock which Margaret immediately envisioned in their garden back home in Missouri, then preceded them into a large rectangular room empty except for a young black girl in an eighteenth-century cotton housedress who smiled at them briefly before resuming sweeping the hearth of the massive fieldstone fireplace with an old-fashioned handmade broom.

Margaret and Raymond followed the librarian across the wide oak floorboards to one of several plain but carefully rubbed and polished wood tables which flanked the split-rail-and-white-plaster-intersticed walls. Above them, shelved pewter serving plates reflected the subdued light from recessed candles; to her left, as she sat down on a low wooden bench, Margaret glimpsed a taproom with a small walnut bar and, against the back wall, massive hogsheads. Everything about the interior of the Ordinary was clean, uncluttered, and redolent of well-tended wood.

"How . . ." Margaret bit off the easy adjectives which rose to her lips and smiled helplessly at her husband and

Taliaferro. "It's a simply *great* room. We should eat here
sometime, Ray; they do serve meals, don't they?"

The librarian's thoughts were obviously elsewhere. He
made no attempt to conceal his concern, but continued to
cast suspicious glances toward the closed door behind the
bar, at the same time absently tapping the tabletop with
the first two fingers of each hand. After an uncomfortable
pause he squinted at his watch, peered nearsightedly
around the room, and clapped his hands smartly. "God!
It's already after three. Where's a waiter or something?"
He started to rise but stopped as a young man in a white
jacket approached from the kitchens. "Ah, thank God.
Three bourbons; doubles." Again he shook his head impatiently, glared at the closed door by the hogsheads in
the bar, and with what seemed a palpable effort turned to
Margaret. "There's a sort of formal dining room, too, out
yonder. It's just for special occasions, banquets, that sort
of thing. But I expect Ray knows as much as I do about
that. He's the historian; I'm just a librarian."

Whether Thorpe's comment was hostile or merely mod-
est, Margaret could not tell, but suddenly she felt extremely uncomfortable. Confined within her body stock-
ing, her flesh beneath the elastic waistband began to itch
and she shifted her position uneasily on the cross-legged
stool: why in heaven's name doesn't Ray say something?
And if Thorpe doesn't stop fidgeting and peering around
the room and at that door so suspiciously, I shall have to
go to the bathroom. Why did Dorsey and Fogel have to
stop *here,* of all places?

"How old *is* the Tavern?" she asked in mild despera-
tion, but then the young man with the drinks was ap-

proaching their table and Thorpe's dour face lightened.
"Cheers," he said, and quickly raised his glass to his lips
and drank deeply. "Cheers to you both. The house,
Margaret, is middle eighteenth-century, but this" — he
waved his hands — "this isn't old at all. It's brand-new,
as a matter of fact. It's on the site of the old Ordinary,
though. But the house, it's the original. Been almost completely restored, of course, and fairly recently too." He
drank rapidly and again glanced around the dim interior.
"As a matter of fact, I've heard there's a new brochure de-
scribing the restoration, the history of the house, and all
that sort of thing . . . Tell you what, I expect I can get
you one. In the gift house — there's one out there — or
the gatehouse. No" — he raised one hand in remonstrance
— "it won't be any trouble." And before Raymond or
Margaret could speak he had risen from his chair, made
a slight bow in Margaret's direction, and left the table,
simultaneously casting a quick sidelong glance at the door
of the taproom.

As the front door closed behind him, Margaret exhaled slowly. "Well, Professor Green, or should I say Historian Green, what's next?"

"He's a real nut, one of the last of the big-time nuts."

"I was really getting nervous, the way he was peering
around. I wish we'd gone straight back to the Boar's Head,
don't you?"

"You can say that again. But you know, I'm beginning
to feel sorry for him."

"I am too, and I like him. He's really awful, but he *is*
funny, and he certainly seems to know his Jefferson. If
he just wasn't so drunk all the time, and so vulnerable

. . . You know, you're the only person who's been decent to him since last night."

"He's been having a rough time, all right. Particularly when Helen Davis snubbed him before lunch; he's always admired Helen, you know. And apparently Dorsey hasn't spoken to him since they picked up Freiberg." Raymond shook his head. "And now . . ."

"You know" — Margaret hesitated — "you know, I'm still a little jealous of Dorsey." *That Dorsey! Damn those long legs of hers and those breasts . . .*

Raymond took a long sip of his drink. "No need to be, we were good friends, Meg, but that was a long time ago."

The faint aroma of freshly baked bread drifted in from the kitchen, the cross-legged bench felt surprisingly comfortable, and from somewhere in the tall pines behind the Ordinary the song of a cardinal broke the midafternoon stillness: *pret-ty pret-ty pretty-pretty.*

"And Thorpe?" Margaret felt like singing too.

"Yeah, Thorpe and Dorsey had something going a few years ago. Not much, but something. Thorpe's not exactly what you'd call a ladies' man."

"And where" — Margaret glanced toward the parking area — "where do you think they are?"

"Dorsey and Freiberg?" Raymond nodded toward the door in the paneled alcove behind the bar. "I expect." He smiled what seemed to her a somewhat forced smile. "I expect they might be upstairs somewhere."

"Do you really think so?"

"How do I know, Meg?" At the trace of harshness in his voice, he reached for her hand. "As I said, Dorsey and I were good friends. When we were in graduate school, but that was a long time ago. And as far as she and our old buddy Freiberg are concerned . . ." He shrugged and grinned. "They may have gone for a bit of a stroll. Berry-picking or something, though it's a bit early in the season for that sort of thing. But the trails are beautiful this time of year." He rubbed the bridge of his nose gently with his index finger. "Or they could be in the gift shop. Buying postcards to take to Mrs. Freiberg. Incidentally, I wonder what's with her and that 'cockerel' spaniel." Raymond half closed his eyes as though in deep thought. "Maybe you were right last night. Maybe something *has* happened to the beautiful Eurasian." He grinned at her wolfishly. "I always thought Freiberg was a criminal type, you know. I imagine he's murdered her. Tossed her body into one of the lakes at the Boar's Head or something."

She started to speak but he pressed her hand, opened his eyes, and for a long moment stared into the semidarkness of the small taproom. "And as for Freiberg and Dorsey, they may simply be upstairs somewhere, fucking."

"Raymond Green! You're simply *awful*. *What* a way to talk!"

He smiled and raised his glass in conscious imitation of the librarian's gallantry. "Do forgive me, Mrs. Green. But first things first, you know."

As Margaret was about to reply, Thorpe Taliaferro entered the room, waving a small folder which he shook open with a flourish. "I got one, you see, brand-new, too." Holding it very close to his glasses, he began to read aloud.

" 'Major John Henry, our famous orator's father, on land granted him in 1735, fashioned this commodious dwelling' — God, what prose that is! — 'the earliest landmark in this vicinity. Major Henry was among the first of the Gentry to occupy his own lands in this part of Virginia. The visitor to the Tavern today, which was sold to John Michie in 1746, is taken back two hundred years to the time Patrick Henry was a young boy. Here many incidents occurred in the boy's life which led' . . . 'which led to his becoming one of the great forces in the American Revolution' . . . 'and to his stinging appeal of "Give me liberty or give me death" delivered at St. John's Church in Richmond.' "

The librarian paused, a frown furrowing his damp forehead; the muscles of his jaws tightened and relaxed and the vein from his left eye to his colorless close-cropped hair writhed like a worm on a hook. He crumpled the pamphlet in one pale hand, threw it angrily to the floor, and sat down heavily beside Raymond.

"Damn that Armistead Davis. That bloody thief."

"What's the matter?" Raymond began, but without deigning to look at him Taliaferro leaned over the table and gingerly, as though it might soil his fingers or burst into flame, retrieved the brochure, uncrumpled it, and tossed it contemptuously to Raymond.

"Ummm, uh, what?"

Thorpe did not reply further but continued to glare at the offending pamphlet before pointing a bony finger. "Look there." He made a wry face as though something had suddenly turned foul in his mouth. " 'Armistead Davis, National Book Award–winning biographer!' Gyahhh! That thing is plagiarized from an article I did three or four years ago. For one of the encyclopedias. *Armistead*

Davis. There ought to be a law against this. Where's that damned boy? I want another drink. You'll have one with me, won't you?"

"Thanks, no." Margaret's response was unhesitating.

"Same here, Thorpe; I'm really exhausted. Too much party for me last night, I guess." Raymond rose from the table. "I think I'd better take a little nap before dinner."

"But can we give you a lift?" Margaret picked up her handbag and stood beside her husband. "Are you sure you don't want to go back to Charlottesville with us?"

The librarian started to shake his head vehemently, but hesitated, stroking his jaw and twirling the ends of his mustaches.

"Forgive me, Margaret," he said finally, while Raymond waited at the door of the Ordinary. "And you too, Raymond. I think maybe I will." He shook his oblong head sadly. "That bastard Davis . . . that's not all he's stolen from me. He's been picking my brains for years, he's a bloody thief, that's what he is. He's stolen from me, he's stolen from Craig, he's . . ."

He tossed off the remainder of his drink and took a step forward, glaring over his shoulder at the taproom.

"I'll be glad to go with you all, if you don't mind stopping at the downtown A.B.C. on the way for some whiskey. To ward off a possible snakebite."

Chuckling harshly, he followed Raymond and Margaret into the slanting sunlight, stopping to glare momentarily at the blue Volvo.

"Those creatures!" he muttered, and squared his shoulders. "And I've got a few more things I want to talk with you about, Raymond. A few more things, if you'll excuse my language, Margaret, about some of these mother-fucking Jefferson scholars that are stinking up the atmosphere around here!"

CHAPTER 9

ANOTHER SIESTA AT THE
BOAR'S HEAD AND A BRIEF
INFORMAL COMMENTARY ON
EIGHTEENTH CENTURY
AMERICAN SOCIAL HISTORY

*The whole commerce between master
and slave is a perpetual exercise of the
most boisterous passions, the most un-
remitting despotism on the one part,
and degrading submissions on the
other . . . The man must be a prod-
igy who can retain his manners and
morals undepraved by such circumstances.* Thomas Jefferson, *Notes on
the State of Virginia,* 1787

"Is any of that true? I mean do you *really* believe all those things Thorpe was saying?"

Margaret's voice was incredulous. She paced the floor of their room at the Boar's Head, pausing occasionally to remove a hairpin or to glance at the white ducks floating lazily on one of the small lakes beyond their window; outside in the lazy peace of the waning afternoon the *pock-pock* of tennis balls against rackets reminded her of Stephen Dedalus listening to the sound of the cricketers at Clongowes Wood, *pock-pock, pock-pock, drops of water falling softly into a brimming bowl* . . .

"What he said about Armistead! And all those horrible things about Martha Jefferson and all the rest! I can't believe that Armistead's a thief, can you? Was *any* of that true? How would Thorpe have found out about it all anyway? And you don't believe what he said about that silly Michie Tavern brochure, do you?"

"No, that's nonsense." Raymond's reply was instant and emphatic. Shoes off, tie loosened, he lay on the great bed in its paneled alcove and appeared to be studying the configuration of the hand-hewn beams of the ceiling. "Nonsense, pure and simple; there's nothing in that brochure you couldn't find in any grade-school history book or tourist guide book. Thorpe's off his rocker far as that's concerned. He did his dissertation on Patrick Henry, you know — I think I mentioned that last night, didn't I? He never was able to get it published, and he's always been, uh, very defensive about it; probably felt that Armistead should have helped him find a publisher, or maybe he thinks Armistead deliberately dragged his feet so he could use some of it himself. But that's unimportant compared to the other things he was saying."

"My goodness, yes." Margaret shook her head slowly and walked to the window, gazing a long moment at the still waters. "It *all* sounded incredible to me. How *could* Thorpe have found out about those manuscripts? And that drawing of Monticello Sally! Surely Craig wouldn't have discussed that sort of thing with Thorpe, would he?"

"Don't ask me, Meg; I shouldn't think so, though. I'm as confused as you are . . . Thorpe's a nut and, as I said, he's paranoid about his dissertation. He's really falling apart; I feel sorry for him."

"So do I, but he's out of sight! Has he always been like that? What was he like? You knew him years ago."

Raymond shrugged helplessly. "We went to the same high school for a couple of years. He wasn't what you'd call popular. Not a weirdo, just not very popular. He'd left Hyattsville when he was eight or nine to go to some prep school, somewhere in New England, I think maybe it was in Connecticut. Then when his father died — he was with one of the banks in Prince Georges County, I don't remember which one — Thorpe must have been fifteen or maybe sixteen then, he came back to Maryland and we finished high school in the same class."

"But what was he *like?*"

. . .

In prep school when he was little Thorpe had always taken the girls' parts oh he was such a beautiful little boy who told me that   I haven't thought of that for years   I remember   it was the wife of the headmaster of Thorpe's prep school in Connecticut   I met her at a reception after I'd given a lecture somewhere and when this woman she was sweet in a nice Edwardian way   a real straight arrow   when she heard I was from Maryland and had gone to Virginia she asked me if I knew Thorpe Taliaferro and when I told her yes she was so delighted   they had all loved little Thorpe she told me   oh what a sweet child he had been she kept saying   what a beautiful little boy and she shook her head and smiled and said what a sweet little thing he was   he always took the girls' parts   no pun intended   that lady had no idea she'd made a pun   little Thorpe always took the girls' parts in the school plays . . .

. . .

"Well" — Raymond rubbed his nose — "he was a good student, and . . ."

"But what was he *really* like? What are you thinking about? What happened after that? After you'd finished high school?"

"Well, after that he went to Johns Hopkins and I went to Virginia, and I don't think I ever saw him for a long time, not until after the army. You wouldn't guess it to see him now, but he had a remarkable service record: a Purple Heart and three Bronze Stars; he was in Korea when I was sitting on my duff in Washington with USAFI . . . So eventually we were both graduate students at Charlottesville. We didn't see much of each other — you know how it is, people from the same high school — we just had a class or two together. He was a good student there, too; brilliant, I guess you might say. He'd made Phi Beta Kappa at Hopkins and I think nothing but A's at Virginia."

. . .

At Virginia he was considered a fag but there were a lot of fairies at the University particularly in the English department and nobody thought much about it one way or the other he was quiet and intelligent and well-mannered and pretty much of a loner and whatever he was up to was his business not mine and I never really got to know him until I went to Woodberry Forest . . .

. . .

"Did he drink then the way he does now? What was he really like, Ray?"

"I guess so, maybe not as much as he does now, but as I said I didn't know him very well at the University. Not until I went to Woodberry Forest; I taught there for a couple of years after I got out of the army. He was there then, too, but teaching English; I think he'd majored in English when he was at Hopkins."

Margaret's eyebrows rose. "Oh, so he did teach at Woodberry Forest?"

"That's right. Three, four years, maybe. Why?"

"Oh," Margaret's voice was casual. "Carla Eppes told me."

Raymond sat up quickly, his eyes angry. "That Carla." He shook his head slowly. "Everybody's friend in need."

· · ·

He came to my room that night to say good-bye   I'm leaving Ray they're kicking me out   they say   I could smell his breath across the room   he was stoned out of his mind   they say I'm a bad influence on the boys   well for God's sake I said sit down man have a cigarette   I wasn't really surprised though   I'd heard some of the kids on the boxing squad joking about him and a couple of the older teachers had made snotty remarks about him now and then but as far as I knew he'd never made any passes at the kids   he kept to himself and whenever possible he'd go away on weekends to Washington or Richmond or anywhere to get away   he had to get away from the school as much as possible he told me once but he never made any passes at the kids or anything like that   he was a good teacher   that's about all I knew   sit down I said sit down and have a cigarette but he just stood there in the doorway swaying   so after a few minutes I fixed some coffee and he sat down and drank it but didn't say anything   look I said   he was beginning to get on my nerves I'm sorry as hell to hear about this is there anything I can do but he shook his head and just kept sitting there so in a little while I said I wish there was something I could do but look man I've got a set of papers to grade and we've got a boxing match coming up this weekend

*good luck hang on in there I'll be seeing you let's keep
in touch all that crap and he put down his coffee cup and
came over and shook hands and left   I wish I'd been more
friendly more sympathetic   I wish I could have helped
him   I wish to God I could have done something for him
but . . .*

．　．　．

"Carla said," Margaret continued, "that Thorpe had
been kicked out because he was a homosexual. Only she
used a . . . shall we say a less academic term."

"That bitch!" Again Raymond shook his head slowly.
"She shouldn't have said that. Sure," he added hastily,
"I guess he was, or is, but he wasn't, as far as I know, hurting anybody. He never made any passes at any of the boys,
I'd've heard about it if he had. I mean what the hell.
Who cares if he was or wasn't as long as he wasn't using
his position to make any of the boys? Only thing, Carla
shouldn't say things like that. How'd she bring it up anyhow?"

"Ray, the woman's mad . . . absolutely . . . well, no,
mad's not the word . . . venomous would be more like
it. I was just standing there on the Terrace, waiting for
you and Craig before lunch. Just standing there, minding
my own business. No, that's not quite true, I was thinking
about Dorsey Jack Morgan and I was so anxious for you to
be with me — I hate being alone at things like that —
and, well, Carla came up and in five minutes she'd dug her
fangs into everybody. Let's see, she'd been talking about
the way Thorpe had acted last night. 'Mista' Eppes,' she
said, 'had been *outraged,* simply *outraged.*' Then Thorpe

had sort of started to come toward us, as if wanting to talk, but Carla looked the other way, and he backed off. 'That *fairy,*' she said, 'you know he was fired' . . . actually she said, 'kicked out on his ass,' but she pronounced it *ahss* — oh, Ray, she's something else — and then she was just starting out on the details when Mr. Eppes came up and steered her away somewhere."

"She's a damned nuisance, really, always into everybody's business. She's on Craig's back half the time, telling him how to run Monticello; she's been calling him constantly the last ten days or so, reminding him to do things he's already taken care of. Nothing suits her, you know. Incidentally, Craig said he might drop by for a drink on his way to the dinner meeting of the Foundation Board . . ."

"Poor Craig! He really has his hands full."

"You can say that again. You know how fussy he is — maybe I should say how, uh, meticulous — you know, he plans these Founder's Day things like a military operation. Begins the next one as soon as the current one's over. Then things start to fall apart." He shook his head. "Like first Thorpe, then Freiberg, then Dorsey falling into the pool. But worst of all is Armistead. Craig's worried to death about what he'll say tonight."

Margaret raised her eyebrows. "But don't you think that's a little foolish of him? To worry so? After all, Armistead's . . ."

"Yeah, I guess so. But he's got no confidence in him anymore, ever since he found out about that Sky Room business. And a public lecture's no place for a lot of stuff about Sally Hemings and — "

"Does Armistead know that Thorpe knows all these things? I still can't believe half of them, can you? What *do* you think about what he said about Sally Hemings and Jefferson? And Martha?"

"Hey, hold on, wait a minute. Let me catch my breath and fix us a drink. Just a little one, huh?"

"All afternoon I've been dying to know what you really think about all this and now you tell me to wait a minute . . . Of course, dear, do mix us a drink, and talk while you're doing it, and I'll do my hair."

Raymond rose from the bed slowly, his forehead creased in thought. "That's crazy, what he was saying about Martha. Jefferson *was* a possessive father, sure. And he had what I guess you'd have to call an unnatural interest in Martha. And she in him. But incest?" Revolving his shoulders irritably, he walked slowly to the dressing alcove, paused, and turned to Margaret. "No, absolutely not. Thorpe's off his rocker there. It's true, though, what he said about Jefferson causing difficulties between Randolph and Martha. But it wasn't deliberate, I'm sure. Lord, Meg, it all gets too Freudian for me . . . Randolph admired Jefferson, there's no question about it. But he was as kinky as hell; there's no question about that, either. He began to feel like an outsider; he thought that Jefferson was comparing him unfavorably with his other son-in-law, and that Martha was comparing *him* with Jefferson, that sort of thing. He wrote a pathetic sort of letter to Jefferson; spoke of himself as the 'silly bird' that could never really be at ease among the swans, that sort of thing. But he never hated Jefferson. Thorpe's wrong there, too."

His shoulders squared, Raymond reached for the whiskey bottle. "Thorpe's wrong about a lot of things, Meg. But as for Sally Hemings and Mrs. Jefferson, that's something else again. He's right about that."

"Really! I'm surprised to hear you say that."

Raymond smiled. "I wouldn't have believed it a few years ago, either. But John Wayles, Jefferson's father-in-law, it's generally known that he had several illegitimate children by a black woman . . . or women."

"Oh?"

"Yeah, it's become more and more obvious in recent years that there was a lot more black-white creep-mousie stuff going on in the South than most 'respectable' white Southerners — including some of my own family — were ever willing to admit. Even Craig — and you know how conservative *he* is, he'd want to kill anybody who said he could *prove* all this — even he's convinced that Mr. Wayles was Sally's father, and Lord knows who else's, even though he wouldn't admit it last night. That's as far as I'll go, though. I don't believe, and no one can make me believe, that Sally Hemings was Jefferson's mistress or whore or concubine or whatever you want to call her, or that any of those children of hers — she had seven or eight eventually — were Jefferson's."

"But who then . . . ?"

Raymond returned with the drinks, shaking his head vehemently. "You know, Meg, I've never tried to make a saint out of Jefferson. No, I haven't" — at the faint smile on Margaret's face he raised a slightly admonishing hand. "He's one of the truly great men of history, but . . ."

"But Sally, who was she?"

"A lot's been written about her lately, since that little

article of mine. Snow Willoughby, of course, is working on her, but her stuff hasn't been published yet. The best account's in Dumas Malone's biography and in one of Merrill Peterson's books on Jefferson, and of course Armistead's. As for Sally, it seems her grandfather was an English sea captain and her grandmother a black African. You might say" — and he raised his glass to Margaret — "that they met on the ship coming over. She had a lot of mulatto children, and some of them, including Sally's mother — Betty — belonged to John Wayles; and some of *them* — this gets pretty complicated, Meg — came to Monticello some time after Jefferson and Martha Wayles — she was a widow, Martha Wayles Skelton — were married. Part of her dowry."

"Hmmmm. How old was Sally then? What was she like?"

"I don't really know . . . that's one of the things I had in my article. Sally was the youngest of Betty's children, at that time anyhow, but she may have been born at Monticello. All I really know is that she was in her early teens, fourteen or maybe fifteen, when she came to Paris with Jefferson's younger daughter, and that was in the summer of . . ." He closed his eyes a moment, brow furrowed in thought. "Summer of seventeen eighty-seven, I think. That's when it all began, some of the 'experts' think, when she came to Paris. But there's no proof. A lot of conjecture and some wild theorizing, but no real proof."

"But . . ."

"Lord, Meg, everybody's tried to debunk Jefferson at one time or other. They called him a coward during the Revolution, but it wasn't till he was running for President —

it was the campaign of eighteen hundred, against Burr, one of the dirtiest ever, maybe worse even than the time Roosevelt was said to have black blood, or like nineteen twenty-eight, when the underground press was saying that Al Smith would sell America down the river to the Pope. It was then, and during Jefferson's first term, that the smear campaign really began. There was a journalist named Callender — a psychopath — he was the one who started the whole Black Sally business, the Jefferson-who-dreamed-of-freedom-in-a-slave's-embrace routine. It became a terrible scandal; everybody got into the act, even John Quincy Adams's been said to have written a ballad about Jefferson and Sally."

He paused and carefully set his empty glass on the windowsill.

"Sally was a beauty, apparently; even Jefferson's grandson — the one who had concealed the Cosway letters, remember? — said she was 'decidedly good-looking.' And could pass for white, I guess. And, as I said, she'd been with Jefferson in Paris and she did live in the White House — the *White* House, get it? — during his presidency. That's supposed to be funny, according to some of the muckrakers."

"It's an amazing story. But, Ray, if Sally *wasn't* his mistress . . . or if Jefferson *wasn't* the father of her children . . . then who was?"

"I'm not sure. What I mean is, I don't know. Some people, including Armistead — at least he used to; maybe he's found something in the Dome Room that's caused him to change his opinion — think it might've been Peter Carr. He was Jefferson's favorite nephew; his mother was one of

Jefferson's sisters and his father had been Jefferson's closest friend when they were boys. He may have been the father of some of them; as I said, Sally had a lot of kids."

"*Some* of them!"

"It wasn't exactly the Age of Enlightenment, Meg." Raymond shook his head slowly. "Or the Age of Reason, either. God in heaven, Meg, can't you see?"

"See? See what?"

"How it must have torn Jefferson apart, all this? Realizing this, knowing this sort of thing was going on under his own roof. As I said before, it wasn't *just* a matter of right and wrong, though that had a lot to do with it. Jefferson *was* a man of principle, God knows. He *did* believe in equality and freedom, and dignity, too, for the individual. Or the *idea* of all that. But he honestly did think that Negroes were inferior to whites, racially, anthropologically, historically . . . All you have to do is read the *Notes on Virginia*: it's all there, and that's where a lot of the muckrakers make their mistakes. They draw their conclusions on, uh, incomplete or misleading premises, or false premises, or circumstantial evidence. They simply don't understand Jefferson the man. Who the hell do they think Jefferson was? Warren Gamaliel Harding? Or F.D.R.?"

At Margaret's frown, Raymond waved his hands airily.

"O.K., O.K., we won't go into that. But to get back to what I was saying: ideas are one thing, facts are another. It's true that Jefferson favored Sally Hemings. *And* her brothers and sisters. But, again, that doesn't really *prove* anything. They were the chosen ones at Monticello, no question about it. And they were smart as whips, some of them. Talented, too; as Mrs. Pennyfeather told you, it was one of Sally's brothers, John, I think it was, who is said to have made some of those Sheraton side chairs — there's at least a couple of them at Monticello. I expect he's the one who's supposed to have made that drawing of Sally Thorpe was talking about. If there *is* such a drawing."

"Incredible!"

"And some of Sally's children were apparently very light skinned, even lighter than she was. 'Bright,' it was called in those days. They were bright, all right, in more ways than one. Lord Almighty, there must have been mulattos and quadroons and octaroons all over the place! One of Sally's sons, it's been said, looked so much like Jefferson that visitors to Monticello commented on the resemblance. He was a butler or Jefferson's personal body servant; I can't remember his name but he and some of the others were freed after Jefferson died — it was in his will. Sally wasn't, incidentally; he left this up to Martha, to avoid heating up the controversy after his death, I guess . . . She wasn't freed till a couple of years after he died."

"So there *is* a lot of evidence?"

"Sure, circumstantial evidence, that is." Raymond stroked his nose thoughtfully. "One of Sally's children, name of Madison Hemings, years later, almost fifty years after Jefferson's death, claimed that his mother had had half a dozen children by Jefferson, and that they had passed for white. Professor Willoughby makes a lot of that, of course. But I think I can prove that the Madison Hemings's story was ghostwritten. When I get *that* article written, I'll really pull the rug from under her. Imagine! Basing a whole elaborate theory on statements made by a drunk like Callender, and a crackpot or liar fifty years after the fact! Phew!"

Raymond wiped his forehead, exhaled mightily, and glanced at his watch. "Lord, Meg, we'll have to hurry. Time for me to get off the soapbox, honey; hope I haven't bored you with all this."

"Are you crazy?" Margaret rose from the bed, her dressing gown parting. "It's a fascinating story. I can see that I've got a lot of reading to do when we get home." Facing the mirror and beginning to arrange her hair, she regarded Raymond's reflected image. "And how does the rest of the cast, Mrs. Cosway and Martha and Colonel Randolph, how do they fit into this picture?"

"I guess someone like Professor Willoughby will 'prove' that the Colonel was the father of all those children. That's about the only thing some of those jokers haven't come up with yet. But Dorsey probably knows more about him and Martha than anybody. Dorsey . . ."

Damn Dorsey . . . "Does Dorsey know about those manuscripts? Or the portrait of Sally? I'd certainly love to see *that,* if it exists. And Craig? What did he say about it?"

"Nothing, actually." Raymond shook his head. "He *does* have his hands full. On top of everything else, Helen's on the warpath. You think Carla's about to explode! That's not a circumstance compared to Helen. She's . . . Craig told me this" — he hesitated — ". . . she's in an uproar about Dorsey, and irritated with him for inviting her."

Margaret turned quickly, dropping her comb to the

dresser with a clatter, and Raymond held up his hand. "I know you don't think too much of . . . I mean Dorsey's really a good person."

. . .

Dorsey   Dorsey   that spring afternoon twenty could it have been twenty years ago I asked her if she'd like to have a beer as we were filing out of Armistead Davis's seminar   it was the first time I'd ever said more than hello Miss Morgan or how are you though we'd been students sitting around the same seminar table every Tuesday afternoon since the end of January   there were very few women graduate students in history in those days and for the most part the male students ignored them   she was as thin as a rail and only mildly attractive then   her real beauty did not come till some years later   she wore her hair very short and straight almost like a man's and she was an excellent student who kept her mouth shut unless Armistead Davis specifically directed a question to her   and then speaking very slowly she would answer succinctly and very intelligently her eyes studying her finger tips the color rising slowly in her cheeks and there would be tiny drops of moisture on her upper lip and the bridge of her nose yes she replied surprised but without hesitation that would be very nice and we walked out of the Graduate House and onto the Lawn   it was late afternoon and everything was very quiet except for some rooks which were circling around the blue-green dome of the Rotunda and squawking as though birds were going out of style and at the far west end of the Lawn the sky behind Cabell Hall was slowly dyeing the green terraces cranberry and after the long winter the Lawn itself had suddenly come back to life green green green except that every few yards it was dotted with small conical piles of manure   every spring and usually just a day or two before the Easter Week dances a two-wheeled cart manned by an ancient Negro with a pitchfork and drawn by a flop-eared mule would toss a mixture of straw and manure over the surface of the Lawn   the undergraduates were always bitching because it ruined Easter Week they said   we sat on the white steps of the Rotunda and watched the sun sink behind the colonnades and then we got up and walked slowly past the Serpentine Walls and down the Long Walk not saying very much and I wondering why I had asked her   we had a glass of beer at the Corner at the Cavalier the first bock of the season ice-chill and full-bodied and delicious and without really thinking about it I asked if she would like to have a drink at the apartment I shared with Craig Babcock and she had agreed   as I followed her through the shadowy hall and up the curving stairway   in many a still-handsome house on this tree-shaded street maiden ladies of impeccable background occasionally rented rooms or small apartments to graduate students   my heart began to beat rapidly and my hands were beginning to sweat as I unlocked the door   fortunately Craig was not in he was probably at the gymnasium lifting weights or jogging majestically around the track and the apartment was fresh and sweet-smelling of spring flowers from the garden below   Dorsey tall and slender and self-possessed quite unlike the shy and quiet student of the seminar sat down on the couch beneath the black-framed woodcut of the East Front

*of Monticello   I asked her would she like a drink   yes
she nodded but when I returned from the small kitchen
with two glasses of bourbon and tap water and no ice the
apartment did not have a refrigerator   Craig and I had
bought an old-fashioned wooden icebox at the secondhand
store on Vinegar Hill we had paid ten dollars for it but
seldom used it except to keep our laundry in it   she had
flushed with embarrassment for the first time since we
had left the seminar I'm awfully sorry she said but I mis-
understood you I never drink spirits   spirits!   I had not
heard the word since I had taken Dean Wilson's course in
the English novel   I'd fix you a coke I said but I have no
ice   a Coca-Cola without ice would be fine she said so I
drank both the whiskeys and tap water while she sipped
her lukewarm Coke and the light faded from the room
when we had finished our drinks I put the empty glasses
on my desk and sat down on the couch beside her and put
my arms around her   she returned my kisses willingly
but not passionately at first and she made no effort to remove my hands but when I started to undo the button at
the back of the blouse   she was wearing a white blouse of
some sort beneath a pale green pullover sweater   she stirred
and half rose from the couch   please she said with a curious dignity which made me feel like a clown please not
quite so fast   we became very good friends from that time
on   two or three times a week she would meet me at the
Cavalier after my 12:30 class in American History the first
class I ever taught and we would have lunch together   every
week or so after we'd been studying we would go to a
movie Craig with us occasionally sometimes to the University Theater where around 10:30 the Chesapeake and*

*Ohio would rumble across the bridge so loud we couldn't
hear the dialogue or sometimes we'd go downtown to the
Lafayette or the Jefferson for an oldie or a rerun   it had
been at the Jefferson one night in June we had gone to see*
The Phantom of the Opera *and at about the time the phantom was crawling through a transom to abduct the soprano Dorsey with a curious urgency whispered something
in my ear and excused herself   she was gone for quite a
long time so long that I was beginning to wonder and I
reached across the empty seat to tap Craig's arm ques-
tioningly but he shrugged and shook his head and returned
his eyes to the screen where terrible things were beginning
to happen in the sewers beneath the opera house   then
Dorsey came back   could we go home in a taxi she asked
after we had filed out of the building   is anything wrong
I said   usually we walked back to the University but she
only said that she felt slightly sick to her stomach   it was
not till years later when we saw each other at the meetings in Williamsburg and we'd had many drinks together
recalling the old days in graduate school that I suddenly
remembered that summer night at the Jefferson Theater
when we had seen* The Phantom of the Opera   *do you
remember that night we saw* The Phantom of the Opera
*you and Craig and I I had asked   and she had replied
very simply and with the same curious dignity when she
had said please not quite so fast that spring evening in the
apartment so many years before   do I remember* The
Phantom of the Opera *I'll never forget it   I had a mis-
carriage that night in the women's room of the old Jefferson Theater . . .*

.   .   .

Raymond got up from the bed and walked to the window. "These sills are made from marble from a quarry near Monticello," he said without turning to Margaret. "What do you think of that, madam? How does that grab you? Are you impressed?"

"I'm impressed." She stood beside him, placing one arm lightly around his waist. "It's going to be a lovely evening."

He stared thoughtfully at the pond where shadows from the just-beginning-to-leaf willows had faded from the unriffled surface of the water. "Helen even wrote to Craig about it." He sighed and glanced at her as if for help. "That's not like Helen Davis. Those Berkeley women."

She felt again the vague regret of the previous night when she had sat alone by the window brushing her hair and gazing at the arabesques the moon had cast upon the sloping lawns and the still lake. Slowly, abstractedly, as though scarcely aware of her actions, she went to Raymond and unbuttoned his shirt and ran her fingers across his chest and shoulders. Affection and passion engulfed her, tinged with a nameless sadness; almost painfully her nipples were tightening and suddenly she was warm, moist, open.

"Don't tell me about Helen, darling," she heard herself saying, her voice muffled, "or Dorsey either," and she gave him her mouth, the warm tip of her tongue searching for his. *Good God what's getting into me we should come to Virginia more often.* And she shrugged her body impatiently, her dressing gown rustling like palm fronds slipping to the floor. Raymond was fumbling with the hook of her brassiere and swiftly, expertly, with one hand she unfastened it, her breasts swinging free. "Oh, I do love you, Ray, really I do," she was saying, and then the phone on the walnut bed table buzzed and stopped and buzzed again, and she almost upset the lamp as she groped for the receiver.

CHAPTER 10

A FRIENDLY VISIT FROM
THE CURATOR

*My expectations from you are high
. . . Nobody in this world can make
me so happy, or so miserable, as you
. . . To . . . yourself I look to ren-
der the evening of my life serene and
contented. Its morning has been
clouded by loss after loss, till I have
nothing left but you.* Thomas Jefferson to Martha Jefferson, March 28,
1787

"ABOUT THAT SO-CALLED PORTRAIT of Sally Hemings . . ." Craig Babcock rested his great head in one cupped hand and kneaded a ruddy cheek with the other. "Nope, I haven't seen it. I've heard about it — you know, nothing's a secret very long around here — but I'm not convinced there *is* such a drawing. If there is" — and he shook his head vigorously — "that would be a real discovery . . . unquestionably the most important new Jefferson stuff since the Cosway letters. But what else is new, Ray? What else did good old Thorpe tell you?"

Following the curator's phone call Margaret had scarcely had time to slip into her dressing gown, kick her rumpled brassiere beneath the great bed and hastily straighten her hair before Craig was knocking at their door, resplendent in a surprisingly wide-lapeled dinner jacket and a ruffled pale blue dress shirt. "I'm glad you like my party outfit, Meg," he had explained half-smilingly, half-apologetically. "Mrs. Pennyfeather gave me this shirt for Christmas. I feel obliged to wear it every so often and besides, you know, I sort of like it."

Stretched out in the comfortable chair by the window, he gratefully extended his hand as a somewhat shaky Raymond passed him a tumbler of whiskey and water.

"It's been a long day, *viejo,* but I'm beginning to roll with the punches. Things can hardly get much worse, so" — he gestured toward the blue ruffles — "I'm almost starting to enjoy them. Almost, not quite."

"Singing in your chains, Craig, like the sea?"

At the curator's blank look, Margaret waved her hand apologetically. "Just a quotation, Craig. From Dylan Thomas. Forgive me."

"That's about all we need right now." The curator smiled grimly. "From the little I know about him, Dylan Thomas would've had the time of his life here today. But Dorsey and that joker Freiberg — I heard, by the way, about his accident on the mountain . . . it's lucky the little smart-ass — excuse me, Meg — wasn't killed. As I started to say, he and Dorsey are doing their best to replace him. Incidentally, Dorsey really loused things up this afternoon."

"Oh?"

Craig turned to Margaret. "She was supposed to be on local TV this afternoon, an of-interest-to-women program, you know: the only woman Jefferson scholar here for Founder's Day, that sort of thing. But she never showed up. Wouldn't have been so bad if they'd planned to tape it, but this was to be live." He shook his massive head. "Guess I made a big mistake inviting her, but . . ." He looked from Raymond to Margaret.

"Meg knows all about Dorsey, Craig . . . I've been trying to fill her in a little at a time."

Craig smiled and took a grateful swallow. "I'm glad . . . and now Armistead's getting antsy because she's been hanging around with Freiberg . . . yeah, I've already heard about the business at Michie's. And God only knows what he's going to say tonight at his lecture . . . he was still drinking with Rodney when I left the mountain. And people — Carla, that is — are beginning to gossip about *Mrs.* Freiberg." Craig leaned forward, briskly snapped his fingers. "That's what I really wanted to tell you. Carla called up the *Progress* after lunch and the editor called me to tell me."

"Oh God, what about this time?" Raymond shook his head in disgust. "I forgot to tell you that, Meg; among other things, our Carla's a great letters-and-telephone-calls-to-the-editor type."

"You can say that again." The curator leaned back in his chair, his eyes half-closed. "Old-line fascist type. She makes Barry Goldwater look like a liberal. Guess she gets that from Webster. She's opposed to anything new: women's lib, liquor by the drink, creative writing classes in the English Department, black athletes at the University . . . 'The day a black athlete sets foot upon the sacred soil of Scott Stadium the University of Virginia should eliminate its intercollegiate athletic program.' That sort of thing, you name it."

"But what was it about this time?"

"She's complaining about communists again, Ray."

"Oh, for God's sake. *What* communists?"

"Apparently John Rodney . . . she was indignant he was at lunch today."

"She's a bad egg, Craig, forget it. But what about Mrs. Freiberg, what'd she say about *her?*"

"Oh, nothing, really. Just keeps asking about her."

"I do wonder what's happened to her, though." Mar-

garet leaned toward Craig, her forehead furrowed in con-
centration. "I can't help wondering about her myself.
Has Fogel said anything to you about it?"

"Not much. During lunch he mentioned something
about her being indisposed, that's all. And Dorsey said
she was going to try to see her this afternoon or something." Again Craig shook his great head. "That Dorsey
. . . forgive me, Meg, for rehashing old laundry, or whatever. I'm very fond of Dorsey. And I don't give a damn
about her private life. If she wants to shack up with that
little joker, it's all right with me. But not on Founder's
Day, damn it."

"Never on Founder's Day. You've got something there,
Craig." The three of them broke into laughter simultaneously and Craig sank back heavily, absently extending his
empty glass toward Raymond.

"And Helen . . . no thanks, Ray, I expect I've had just
about all I can handle." His large hands performed helpless wringing gestures. "Look, you all, I need your help."
His face darkening, the curator fumbled for his watch. I
will always remember him, Margaret thought, pulling out
that enormous watch, and frowning. "Cock Almighty, it's
later than I thought. See if you can cool things tonight,
will you? Meg, if you can get Dorsey to the lecture, but
not with Freiberg, and to the Colonnade Club for the reception afterward . . . O.K.? And, Ray, keep your eye
on that little smart-ass."

At the door, he paused and a slow smile creased his face.
"That's all for this time, folks. Thanks for the drinks . . .
and for the help. The charades will resume at eight-thirty."
Craig waved his large hands. "I think."

"What was that you were saying last night, about the Mafia and their hangups?" Raymond was smiling as the door closed behind the curator's broad back. "Slightly neurotic, I believe you said. We're a pretty straight group, if you ask me, compared to some of those civilians. That bitch Carla! She's never read a line of Rod's, not even the trilogy. And Fogel Freiberg! Now there's a real citizen for you. He's a poet, of course, though he hasn't written any poetry since he went to *Native Roots* . . ."

"Your prejudices are showing, darling. And I thought you said you were beginning to like him."

"My prejudices? What about *his* prejudices? That poem of his about the University! And about Jefferson."

" 'Jefferson's Dream'? Oh, Ray, that's a fine poem."

Raymond shrugged. "O.K., if you say so. But it's all wrong-headed. Let's see, how does it begin?" He cleared his throat self-consciously and, eyes half-closed, commenced to quote.

> I said: What is University
> Is not my style:
> Keep
> The Kike and Nigger a mile
> Away.
> I say: What
> Is University? Today.

"Raymond, you amaze me. A Southern Conference boxing champion quoting poetry! You never told me."

Smiling in pleased embarrassment, Raymond gently stroked the bridge of his nose. "I started to minor in English, but then I got interested in Jefferson, and . . . well, you know." He shrugged and waved his hands. "O.K., so it's a pretty good poem. But it's not only wrong-headed, it's dishonest. Deliberately dishonest. It, uh, perverts the whole concept of the University. And of Jefferson, too. Fogel Freiberg wouldn't like Jefferson if he were in this room. What does that schmuck know about Jefferson anyhow?"

Margaret shook her head tolerantly.

"'Not my style.' 'Death of dream.' 'Reason betrayed.'" Raymond revolved his shoulders and took a deep breath. "You know where Freiberg was before he went to *Native Roots*? With Time, Inc. For a paltry fifty thousand, Craig told me. Ugh! He should be with *Cosmopolitan. Native Roots* is becoming a nationalistic *Commentary.* With illustrations yet! Freiberg should be writing TV commercials for milk of magnesia."

Again the phone buzzed and Margaret ran swiftly to the bed table. "Hello, oh *hello,*" she said, and at the same time cast Raymond a reassuring smile. "How are you feeling? . . . why . . . how very nice . . . no, we don't . . . just a minute, let me ask Raymond." She placed her hand over the mouthpiece and turned to her husband, whispering. "It's Thorpe. Wants to know if we'll have dinner with him."

God, no. Raymond's stage whisper caused her to raise a hand in warning.

"I'm so sorry, Thorpe. We're both exhausted, and Raymond has a slight headache. It was so nice of you to . . . Yes, we'll probably just have a bite in the room before the lecture. Yes, yes."

Margaret replaced the phone and smiled and came to her husband. Again she put her arms around his waist and her mouth to his.

"He's drunk as a lord," she said. "Drunk as a lord."

CHAPTER 11

THE SCHOOL OF AFFLICTION:
A FUGUE IN SIX PARTS

*Tried myself in the school of affliction,
by the loss of every form of connection
which can rive the human heart, I
know well, and feel what you have
lost, what you have suffered, are suf-
fering, and have yet to endure. The
same trials have taught me that for ills
so immeasurable, time and silence are
the only medicine.* Thomas Jefferson
to John Adams, November 13, 1818

PART 1

ARMISTEAD DAVIS, 5:30 P.M.

*Give up money, give up fame, give up
science, give up the earth itself and all
it contains, rather than do an immoral
act.* Thomas Jefferson to Peter Carr,
August 19, 1785

EVER-PRESENT CIGARETTE in hand, Armistead rose uneasily from the bed. His head was still clouded from
the drinks he had had with John Rodney before the luncheon at Monticello, the calves of his legs were like lead
weights, and his stomach was fluttering; he could not remember ever having felt more fatigued. He glanced at
his wrist watch: almost five-thirty, in an hour he and Helen
and John Rodney were due at the president's house for
dinner. Two or three cocktails would get him through
that ordeal, and then at eight-thirty he would have to
give the Founder's Day address.

He tiptoed to the comfortable chair by the window, carefully avoiding the bed so as not to awaken Helen, who lay
with her head cradled in the crook of one pale arm, her

bluish eyelids flickering ever so slightly; soon, he knew, she would start almost imperceptibly, utter a slight gasp, and slowly open her eyes. I wish she would sleep forever, he thought, but immediately flushed with compassion for the unhappy woman he had lived with for so many years, so many years without trust or love. *How had it happened when had it really begun   the slow slow process of drifting apart   the long long years of deceit and remorse   the reconciliations the meaningless comings together . . .*

He rose abruptly from the chair, shaking himself as though to ward off a swarm of bees: at least it would be good to come back to Virginia and the University, to spend the last years of his professional life where it had begun — *so long ago   forty   could it be forty years   my God I'm becoming an old man   before I know it Professoremeritus Davis will be shuffling down the Lawn to meet his last seminar . . .*

He walked swiftly to the dresser and poured himself a drink from the half-empty bottle of Jack Daniels on the dressing table. Morosely he studied his reflection in the mirror, pressing with his finger tips the slack flesh beneath his chin, and quickly switched off the unkind light. He reached in the pocket of his dressing gown for a cigarette — *where did I lay that last one down   where is that damned holder   did I give it to Helen?*

Back in the bedroom he bent over and studied Helen's face; in sleep the lines of age and worry and frustration had almost disappeared and there was the ghost of youth about her still-patrician features: the slender high-bridged nose, the pale lips drooping ever so slightly at the corners, the slight cleft of her chin. *If we had had children per-*

*haps things might have been different it is bad to be push-
ing sixty-five with no children* . . .

Helen stirred slightly, gently rubbing her forehead with
one pale hand, the slender fingers curled like the petals
of a flower no longer fresh. Her lips barely trembled and
she gasped slightly and opened her eyes. The sleep drained
from her face and the sad lines reappeared: *she is an old
woman, and she hates me.* Without speaking Armistead
turned from the bed and walked to the dresser and quietly,
methodically, drank the whiskey and water.

. . .

*At least I still have the biography   four volumes fin-
ished and two to go   and the last the best of them all   if
I live long enough to write them   the last great years
Jefferson in retirement   the great autumn years   the
founding of the University   the time to sit and think
work and contemplate   watch the sun rise and watch it
set   good God   the letters to Adams alone enough for
immortality if that means anything   a long and a good
life   for the most part anyhow   the dream the pursuit
almost to the end   but then the slow fading the diminish-
ing the aloneness   Maria Maria   the burdens the debts
Martha and Tom   and Sally   bodily decay is gloomy
in prospect but of all human contemplations the most ab-
horrent is body without mind   end quote   an old man
and alone   Maria oh Maria   adieu my very dear friend
be our affections unchangeable and if our little history is
to last beyond the grave be the longest chapter in it that
which shall record their purity warmth and duration   the
church of Santa Maria della Grazie   hic jacet   pious*

religious and devout young ladies gather here to pray for the soul of the baroness Maria Hadfield Cosway widow gone into the hands of God the fifth of January I am closing the last scene of my life fashioning and fostering an establishment for the instruction of those who come after us you and I ought not to die until we have explained ourselves to each other no that's Adams did you ever see a portrait of a great man without perceiving strong traits of pain and anxiety these furrows were all plowed by grief I am ripe for leaving Martha Maria Tom Sally an old woman worth thirty dollars oh those letters those sad sad letters I can no longer stay with shadow stealthily up the hidden stairs what I hold most precious is your satisfaction indeed I should be miserable without it all those children stealthily Thenia Critty Sally and Harriett I am but a goose among swans dear sir stealthily bad bad Peter I have seen enough of grief tried beyond my endurance oh those letters for here more Snopes than Sartoris we are not afraid to follow they'll make the little old bitches sit up and honor honor Dorsey Jack I wish things had been better for you Dorsey Jack

. . .

Her hand on his shoulder was like an electric shock: he started, almost overturning the empty glass; Helen stood before him, pale, all the remnants of her faded beauty erased.

"I suppose I should congratulate you. You have it now, Armistead, haven't you? The Chair, and Dorsey . . . everything you've always wanted."

He looked at her a long time without replying: *this is what it all comes down to an old man and an old woman no love no affection not even the remnants of respect.*

"You might say that, Helen." His voice was dry. "You might say that, but I wouldn't." He started to step past her, but her hand was on his arm.

"I wish I could. I know how much it means to you."

"Don't try," he said, surprised at the hardness in his voice. "It means less than you think."

She stepped back as though he had struck at her, the look in her eyes telling the story:

. . .

They had lived on a tree-shaded street within walking distance of the University grounds the tail end of the Depression a small apartment they paid thirty-two dollars a month for it including maid service they had been married a week he had come home from class earlier than usual the apartment quiet he had tiptoed through the sun-drenched living room to the kitchen intent engrossed Helen was making a pie her first a pecan pie and as he hesitated in the doorway she had reached across the kitchen table for a stick of butter and overturned the glass pie plate shattered into fragments on the tiled floor oh Lord or Lord oh goddamn it was the first time he had ever heard her curse and then she had placed her fair head and her flour-flecked arms on the kitchen table and wept silently he had come up behind her circled her with his arms her breasts beneath the kitchen dress floating free swelling without speaking they had sidestepped the ruins of the pie in the small bedroom

*they made love again and again it seemed as though they
would never grow old later lying hand in hand while
the shadows darkened beneath the mimosa trees outside
their windows she told him it was the first time she had
she tried to say the word she could not say it there was no
need to say it . . .*

. . .

"I'm sorry, Helen," he said. "I didn't mean to sound
like that." Again he fumbled in his dressing gown. "I seem
to have misplaced my cigarette holder; I was looking for
it earlier. Do you have it?" He paused and looked at her.
"And I think we'd better hurry. We're due at the president's house before long. Rod will be waiting for us downstairs. Soon."

"I'm not going with you, Armistead."

"Not going with me? What do you mean, not going?"

"Just that, Armistead, I'm not going."

Exasperated, he returned to the dresser and reached
for the whiskey bottle.

"You drink too much, Armistead."

He shrugged and poured two inches of bourbon into his
glass, added an ice cube, and filled the glass with water
from the tap.

"I wish you'd come, Helen. It will be . . . it will be
awkward if you don't come."

Her voice was as cold as his had been. "It's a little
late for that sort of thing. Don't you think so, Armistead?"

"Late? What sort of thing?"

She did not answer but sat down wearily on the edge of
the bed, her small nipples dark points beneath her slightly

parted dressing gown. He averted his eyes, his heart thumping, and walked to the window: *there is never enough time   I must think about that damned speech   Rod is right I guess . . . I wouldn't do it Armistead   not tonight anyhow   this isn't the time or the place   I wish you would consider   at least I hope you will take out that business about Thomas Mann Randolph and . . .*

"What sort of thing!" Helen's voice was incredulous. "God in heaven, Armistead, how can *you* ask *me* what sort of thing? God forgive you, Armistead, I can't."

He flushed, the pulse pounding in his temples. "I must . . ." He struggled to control his voice, and ran his hand carefully over his cheeks and jaws, as though feeling for some hidden tumor. "I must shave again . . . I need to run the razor over my face."

At the door to the bathroom he paused. "I wish you would come. What will I tell the president? And Rod?"

"Tell them anything you like, Armistead. You're very good at telling people things."

He switched on his electric razor, frustration and anger hardening in his belly; for a moment he felt he could not breathe. He was sweating and the white stubble resisted the razor; he had a sudden impulse to hurl the thing through the window. When his heart stopped thumping he switched the razor off and carefully laid it on the shelf above the basin. Gently he slapped handfuls of cold water on his cheeks and chin, drying his face meticulously before shaking preshave lotion into a cupped hand and patting the foul-smelling liquid upon his skin. He picked up the razor, peering with angry eyes at his reflection, avoiding breathing too closely into the mirror, carefully guiding the razor around his throat and the small patch of white stubble near his Adam's apple which always resisted the razor.

The phone in the bedroom rang and he called, "Helen, will you get that damned phone?" The ringing stopped and above the buzzing he heard her say, "Yes, yes, he'll be down right away, yes, right away." He pressed the razor against his throat, released it angrily and gazed at the stiff white hairs in the mirror. He ground his teeth and closed his hand over the razor and hurled it viciously against the tiled wall.

"That's very adult, Armistead." Helen stood in the doorway, her eyes as contemptuous as her voice. "That's very appropriate for the recipient of the Thomas Jefferson Chair. The man of reason." She paused. "Rod's waiting for you downstairs. He wanted to come up but I told him I wasn't dressed. Your taxi's waiting." She turned on her heel, her back stiff, and he bent down, painfully, to retrieve the shattered razor.

PART 2

THE BOAR'S HEAD INN:
THORPE TALIAFERRO, 7:00 P.M.

I know the difficulty with which a stu-
dious man tears himself from his studies.
Thomas Jefferson to Peter Carr, August
19, 1785

So they don't want to go to dinner with me   "I'm so
sorry Thorpe but we're both exhausted and Ray has a
slight headache so I think we'll just have a bite in the room
before the lecture" . . . *bite in the room eh so that's what*
they call it   that Meg turns me on and she's a sweet thing
too   I'd like to put the horns on good old Raymond but
he's a decent enough guy   he was the only one at Wood-
berry who   at least they weren't invited to the president's
for dinner either   I wonder if Ray remembers   of course
he must   why in God's name did I go to his room that
night   but I had to talk to someone and he was the only
we're sorry Mr. Taliaferro but your services are no longer
what a blow   and just because because because   nothing
absolutely nothing no   I did not I never did   now where
did I put those damned . . .

. . .

He fumbled beneath the pillow for his glasses, finally
retrieving them at the foot of the couch. Comfortable, he

stretched out, dangling one long leg over the edge of the couch, extracted a candy bar from the pocket of his shirt, and carefully unwrapped it.

. . .

Lord I'm hungry   silly not to have gone down to dinner but it's no fun eating alone   I wonder what the Nelsons will be serving Armistead in all his glory   Mr. God Almighty   fuck him   I'll blow the whistle on him by God I will if he ever steals my stuff again   honor code my ass does he really have all that   I doubt it   and he's all wrong about Cosway   so there was some hanky-panky that day in the carriage from Avignon   but not in America not in Washington   he's off his rocker   the Old Stud is off his rocker and a thief too   couldn't keep that sort of thing secret   not with the campaign of 1800   smears yellow journalism   freedom in a slave's hide your Bibles in the rocks baby big daddy's going to burn them burn baby burn   buy your babies chastity journalists yellow journalism   Callender dying in three feet father of yellow   dreamed of freedom in a slave's embrace   Sally was a quadroon   oh my pretty   oh Sally hearken to my vows yield up thy sooty charms my best beloved my more than spouse oh take me to thy arms   no no nasty Jefferson couldn't   Peter Carr   old man Wayles yes but not TJ   Callender worse than Mayor Daley or that shit-ass Agnew   now Martha Jefferson that's another cup of tea papers hidden in sky room stashed away Jefferson too cagey for   but Martha maybe foxy like them all tuck between her legs maybe nonono   daddy's little girl   Colonel Randolph crazy as a loon rode his horse

*from Richmond to Monticello   what was his name
Belvedere   no Duke   no Dromedary that's it Dromedary   wild wild a dozen children Ray said eleven I think
he's wrong Martha ran away   come home to daddy
what a scene   horses straining up mountain   old man in
his study looking at University telescope in tearoom
surprise surprise daddy I'm home   other daughter more
attractive   Martha plain as an old shoe died schooled in
grief yet a real woman too by God   Sully portrait   those
eyes take off your old blue bonnet   bluebonnet plague
old nurse used to say spoonerism no malaprop   except
for fullness of the cheeks spit image of Jefferson   but incest no Dorsey off her rocker there but still she knows
more   women know more than men or do they   Dorsey
Dorsey   night in Williamsburg   couldn't   why Jefferson
didn't   no need to Willoughby says   why marry Sally
Hemings   secret   steps   night   couldn't   get it up
Martha Wayles Skelton   honeymoon cottage   blizzard
marvelous place for Dorsey   fire in fireplace   snowing
servants all gone to sleep   everything dark but fire glow
dark enough candles   slowly take off her   rosy light
long-legged   why couldn't I   still she's a sweet thing
Armistead   that bastard I could kill   what does she see
in Freiberg   long hair ape   Michie's   that blue Volvo
they must have   haven't seen them since lunch   women
that day at the library Carla Eppes fat tits on my arm
pressing still feel them   big tub of guts   still those fat
udders on my arm where could she have   marvelous new
material   where   could   she   have   found   out   Dorsey
wouldn't tell   or would she   Freiberg wants her to do*
Native Roots *why couldn't I   God knows I wanted*

wonder if she ever told Armistead no she wouldn't wish I hadn't talked so much Green and his wife still he's a decent chap but worships Armistead that sexy little wife Middle Western novelist who killed Roger Ackroyd former boxer in this corner why did I talk so much Woodberry Forest Sally Hemings plagiarism steal my stuff my thanks to Dorseyjack-Morgan early American history without whose would she Armistead can't live forever oh Mr. Tollivuh we understand that night in Williamsburg she'd never tell him Thomas Jefferson Chair of History I have some-thing none of them knows not fat tits not Armistead not Dorsey not Craig Babcock Xeroxed lock and key wait till that's out old black folder red ribbon turned to dust when I touched it Library of Congress and Armistead thinks he's got it all Dome Room Martha Colonel Randolph poor old Babcock thinks he knows every inch under the plaster who'd think it terrible of Armistead not to immediately Babcock bigcock took him for a ride oh Mista Tollivuh Dorsey Freiberg why Dorsey Jews what's happened to Mrs. Freiberg I hate women like that Jews cat in a sack don't Dorsey not with Freiberg what did I say to Greens too much to drink where are the graves of the two thieves blue Volvo that sexy little Midwestern wife would she what did I tell him in the head last night Armistead thief he worships him would he tell where Dorsey Freiberg horseydorsey those small tight they're the best would she tell?

.   .   .

The librarian stretched his long legs and yawned, his back had a crick in it, and he turned painfully onto his side, stretched again, and sighed in relief. He nibbled a morsel of the chocolate, savoring the sweetness, then carefully gathered the last succulent crumbs from the palm of his hand and deposited them in the wastepaper basket.

Would she would she would she?

PART 3

THE AMPHITHEATER: RAYMOND AND MARGARET, 9:55 P.M.

Think of me much, & warmly. Place me in your breast . . . & comfort me. Thomas Jefferson to Maria Cosway, December 24, 1786

WITH DIFFICULTY Raymond picked his way down the crumbling steps of the amphitheater. "Be careful," he said, extending a hand toward Margaret. "The place isn't what it used to be; it looks as though it's falling apart."

Halfway down, he bent over and brushed the bone-gray surface with his finger tips; from the hard, cold stone powdery dust rose slowly to his nostrils. He took Margaret's arm and they sat down, gingerly, close to each other. Behind them, beyond the Serpentine Walls and the sweet-

scented gardens of the pavilions on the Lawn, the sky
glowed faintly above the pediment of Cabell Hall where
the remnants of Armistead Davis's audience still lingered
on the broad steps; in front of them tall black pines bord-
ered the remains of what had been the stage of the amphitheater.

"You couldn't tell by looking at it now." Raymond gestured toward the once-grassy arena. "By God, they're making a parking lot out of it or something. But they used to
have open-air concerts here, and occasionally a play, that
sort of thing. Craig played Falstaff up there, when we were
in graduate school."

He turned his eyes from the crumbling platform,
breathed heavily, and leaned over to rub the calves of his
legs. "Ugghhh! I used to run up those steps, every day
when we were in training. We used to have to get up every
morning around six and do roadwork . . . down there,
near the foot of Lewis Mountain, you can't actually see it
from here, we'd head up that hill and then up here and
then back down." He stretched out his legs and groaned
again. "It tires me out just to think about it; you must
make me start working out again, Meg, when we get back
to our prairie home."

*An unquiet ghost walks at Monticello at midnight
. . .* Armistead Davis had begun, *a restless ghost.* He *was*
a spellbinder, Margaret had had to admit to herself —
handsome, dynamic, assured, and with just enough of the
circuit rider's theatricality to entertain the people who
had just come along for the ride. He had talked eloquently,
persuasively, of the need to reevaluate The Founder in
terms of present-day realities, of the need to rescue the man

from the myth. And then he had lowered his voice, and spoken of *important new discoveries, revelations necessitating a rewriting of The Founder's private life,* and Margaret could sense Raymond's sudden tension as well as her own. But then, really, to all intents and purposes, Armistead had stopped: the remainder of his talk seemed even to her something she had heard or read many times before, beautifully organized, splendidly delivered, and enthusiastically applauded, but containing nothing which seemed either original or even illuminating . . .

"I guess Craig can sleep more easily tonight, don't you? What did you really think of the speech?"

Raymond locked his fingers and cracked the joints noisily. As usual after a lecture or a concert he felt strangely inarticulate and awkward; it took him time to sort out his thoughts, clear his head, get his blood and his mind working freely again.

"Let's face it," he said, finally. "It was pretty much of a bust. I'd been expecting too much, I guess. All the talk and rumor about new discoveries." Raymond sighed and stretched out his legs; the moon had floated behind the clouds and the amphitheater was suddenly quite dark; behind the semicircle of silent stone only the base of Lewis Mountain remained visible. "Something happened to make him change his mind. I wish I knew what it was. Of course, if some of the 'discoveries' are as important as people seem to think they are . . . if they're that good, he'll probably want to hold them till the last volume of the biography. *If* he lives to finish it."

"*If?* Aren't we being awfully morbid tonight?"

"No, not really." He looked gloomily at the dark sky,

locked his fingers, and again cracked the joints. "Armistead must be close to sixty-five. And it's taken him, good Lord, almost twenty-five years to do the first four volumes. It's really pretty spooky, but since Randall no one's — not even Dumas Malone — ever finished a really good biography of Jefferson. And there's never been a first-class study of his last years: there're lots of good things been done on his political philosophy or his career as a statesman, that sort of thing, but never a really good study of his mind, his private life, and all that, particularly after he retired from the presidency. They're the years that really interest me. That's what I really want to do a book on later, when I know a lot more about them, those last years. I guess they're the ones Armistead wants to get into, too, particularly now with those new papers and everything." He shook his head and flexed and unflexed his fingers. "Seems to me the older Jefferson got, the greater he became. But they were bad years, too, of course; hellish in some ways. All the trouble with Thomas Mann Randolph — as Thorpe said, he even poker-whipped one of his sons-in-law, *at* Monticello, mind you — and that Sally Hemings business, and the debts, and God knows what-all. But somehow the old man never lost his spirit; you must read those late letters of his to John Adams, they'll break your heart. His mind was like the house, you know, so complex but, uh, so spacious." Raymond sighed and removed his glasses, scrutinizing them as though seeking to decipher a message. "He, uh, I think that's what Aristotle meant by magnanimity, or harmony."

"I think that's it." Margaret propped her chin in one hand and placed the other in Raymond's lap. "I could feel it this afternoon, at the house. I'm beginning to understand the way you feel about Jefferson. For the first time."

"Chastellux." Raymond stared into the darkness. "Chastellux, he was a French soldier and writer, visited Monticello once. He said something to the effect that Mr. Jefferson's mind, like his house, was on a mountaintop . . . Forgive me, honey, I'm the bromide king again tonight; it must be all the drinks."

"You are *not* the bromide king. Or, if you are, let's have more bromides. Mind on a mountaintop. I like that. That's damned good, Ray; it makes a lot of sense." She leaned over and kissed him. "And I can match it."

"Oh?"

"Do you remember what Henry James said about Hawthorne?"

"Henry James? Hawthorne? No, I don't remember. Matter of fact, I don't believe I ever knew it."

"James said" — she wrinkled her forehead — "that anyone attempting a portrait of Hawthorne had to — had to use a very fine brush. Or pencil or something of the sort. Seems to me that that could be said of any Jefferson biographer. A very fine brush. That's what — how shall I say it without sounding like a prig? — that's what, oh hell, that's what rather shocked me here."

"Shocked you?"

"Maybe that's too strong. Let's say surprised me. You know, honey, I've read what you've written on Jefferson, and I've heard you talk about him, shall we say, quite a lot?"

"You might say that." He grinned in the darkness.

"And I've heard you talk about these people. You

know, Armistead, and Webster Eppes, and all the rest.
And now, now meeting them." He started to interrupt, but
she raised her hand. "Oh, I've had the same experience
before. Before we were married. With writers. Poets or
short-story writers or novelists whose work you respect and
when you meet them they turn out to be bores or drunks,
or they spill drinks and ashes on your best rugs or throw
up in the bathroom or make passes at somebody's mother.
That sort of thing. But the Mafia! I'm not really naive but
I guess I thought that somehow, spending their lives working on Jefferson, some of that harmony and magnanimity
might have rubbed off on them a little more than it has.
And there's an awful lot of hostility in the air, Ray: remember the way Carla was glaring at Armistead before
lunch?" She shook her head. "They're interesting, all
right, I'll say that for them. But harmony? Magnanimity?
Uh-*uh*. It's a pretty screwed-up bunch, darling, if you ask
me."

Raymond smiled and lifted a hand in conscious imitation
of Carla Eppes. "Please, my *deah,* rememba' wheah you
are . . . You're a great woman, Meg; and I thought I was
the sentimentalist of the family."

"I'm serious, Ray; you know, all day, I've been feeling
that something's going to happen. I've been thinking of
Mauve, too; you think I'm loony, I know, but something really may have happened to her, and I'm going to
try to find out. Your old buddy Craig may have more on
his hands than either of you bargained for."

"Wild, wild," Raymond said, and squeezed her hand.
"What a business! And speaking of Craig, we'd better get
going." He glanced at the luminous face of his watch.

"Christ Almighty, we'd better get a move on, or Craig *will* start falling apart."

"He's a sweet guy, all right." She rose slowly, brushed the dust from her skirt, and started up the crumbling steps of the amphitheater. "There's such openness about him, Ray; I don't see how he gets along with some of those . . ." Her voice trailed away, and when she spoke again it was more to herself than to her husband. "He believes in what he's doing, and it shows in the way he talks and the way his face lights up when you ask him how high the risers are on the steps at Monticello or how many mulberry trees Jefferson planted in a certain year." She paused momentarily to catch her breath and turned to Raymond. "He respects Jefferson and he believes in him and, damn it, it *has* rubbed off on him. In his own little — or big — way, his mind's on a mountaintop, and so is yours, and I'm glad you and he are such close friends, and I love you both."

Raymond turned and faced her, awkwardly fumbling with the lapels of his dinner jacket. After a long pause he put his arms around her; overhead an airplane droned, green and red wing lights winking in the dark sky, and disappeared beyond the mountains. "I appreciate that, Meg. I appreciate that very much." He kissed her and took her hand. "It's getting chilly," he said, and buttoned his dinner jacket and turned up the collar. At the last tier they stopped, turned, and looked down across the gray bowl of steps. Beyond the ruined stage, lights were flickering at the base of Lewis Mountain. They turned again, sidestepping some rubble, and walked slowly along the winding tree-lined path that led back to the Lawn.

PART 4

WEST LAWN: THE EPPESES, PAST MIDNIGHT

*Subdue your passions, or they will trans-
form you into a beast.* Thomas Jefferson
to Thomas Mann Randolph, December
20, 1800

AT THE DOOR to their pavilion Webster Eppes stood aside,
fumbling for his key and ignoring Carla, who twice had
tried to slip her arm through his as she had followed
him unsteadily across the Lawn from the Colonnade Club.
"Oh Web," she had giggled, "let's go sit on the steps, jus'
a few minutes, please," and she had gestured toward the
Rotunda glowing like a cinnamon and vanilla fantasy at
the east end of the Lawn. "It's such a luvlee night."

But he had turned without speaking and walked stiffly
across the damp grass, his heart fluttering. His irritation
at Carla's behavior at the Colonnade Club had left him
almost literally breathless; only now, as he inserted a large
brass key in the lock, could he breathe comfortably again.
But in spite of his anger he felt, as always, a surge of pride
as he surveyed the handsome facade of their pavilion:
designed by Mr. Jefferson himself for the first professors
when the University had opened its doors almost a century
and a half ago, a pavilion on the Lawn remained one
of the most coveted residences at the University of Virginia. Webster straightened his thin shoulders as his eyes

lingered lovingly upon the graceful recessed doorway with its handsome brass knocker and matching plate engraved in Edwardian script: *Pavilion G, The Eppeses.* At least they can't take this from me, it's ours, mine, till I retire — Jefferson Chair or no Jefferson Chair.

He turned the massive key and stood aside for Carla, who hesitated, one hand on the doorknob, looking at him pleadingly, but he averted his eyes and made a coldly peremptory gesture. Inside the entry hall, weaving ever so slightly, she turned to him again, but he locked the door without looking at her and switched off the brass lamp on the walnut table.

"Go upstairs, please. I'll be along later."

"Oh Websta'." Carla swayed uncertainly, trying to brace herself against the newel post at the foot of the narrow stairs. "Ah'm sorry, b'leeve me, ah'm so sorry." She took a tentative step toward him but he halted her with an uplifted hand.

"You've had too much to drink," he said. "You're drunk. And disgusting." At her look his voice softened ever so slightly. "I don't want to talk, Carla, please go up and go to bed. I'll be up in a few minutes."

He turned and walked slowly along the narrow corridor and through the high-ceilinged dining room, its crystal chandelier, mahogany table, chairs, breakfront, and china closet austere in the dim light. How handsome it all is! He shook his head sadly and entered the kitchen, stubbing his toe on the loose floorboard beyond the doorsill. *Carla, Carla, how many times have I asked you to get this fixed we must call the building and grounds people today no too busy not today but tomorrow.* He switched on the

ceiling light, wincing in the sudden glare. Almost mechan-
ically he prepared a cup of Ovaltine; an insomniac, he
found the kitchen a refuge from the gray terrors of sleepless nights, and often tiptoed downstairs to sit there and
think, enjoying something warm to accompany the one
or two Equanils he invariably took at bedtime, waiting for
the delicious sense of drowsiness, waiting for rest.

His hand shook as he carefully measured a heaping
tablespoon of the dark granules into the china mug with
the now blurred drawing of the Rotunda. Affectionately
he patted the mug their son Wayne had given him for
Christmas — *ten could it have been ten years ago   the
lost boy   the boy they saw only during his vacations from
Woodberry Forest* . . . "How can you all stand it," he
had complained last Christmas, "living on the Lawn
like this? It's like living in a zoo, I hate it."

At the furry smell of the almost-boiling milk he clumsily
picked up a potholder from the magnetized hook at the
side of the electric stove and gingerly removed the pan from
the heat. He poured the milk carefully into the mug, at
the same time briskly stirring the contents. Then he rinsed
out the saucepan before leaving it, water-filled, in the sink
for the maid, turned off the stove, and returned to the
kitchen table with the cup, gratefully inhaling the aroma
which always reminded him of his childhood: his mother
had been a great believer in Ovaltine . . . *Mother poor
Mother was her life as gray as mine   what must it have
been like married to a half-crazy hypochondriac asso-
ciate professor at Randolph-Macon   and his father chairman of the Board of Visitors   portrait still hangs in the
Graduate House as strong a man as father was weak   bad*

*living in the shadow of someone so much better   it's Tom
and Martha all over again* . . .

He loosened his black bow tie and switched off the
ceiling light. In the spacious screened-and-glassed back
porch he sank gratefully into his favorite rattan chair.
The walled garden between their pavilion and the rear of
the West Range dormitories was murky and indistinct,
the moon had long since set, and beyond the Range only
an isolated wink of light from one of the houses on Lewis
Mountain pinpointed the darkness: too many houses
there now. *I can remember when there was only the mansion at the summit.* He took a sip of Ovaltine and withdrew a flat white disk from the leather pillbox he always
carried with him. Carefully he set the mug on the floor,
and placed his hand, palm down, against his chest: you
should go easy on those Equanils, Webster, his doctor had
told him, particularly when you've had quite a lot to drink.
Reassured at the slow steady movement of his heart, he
placed the pill carefully on his tongue, as far back as possible; sometimes a pill would stick halfway down his throat
and he would suffer agonizing visions of choking, stran-
gling — *after all hadn't Sherwood Anderson   it was Anderson wasn't it   died with a sliver of a toothpick in his
throat at a cocktail party or something   Panama City
Havana* . . . ?

He gagged, his pulse quickened, his heart made its
too-familiar stutterlike fluttering descent. He grabbed for
the mug and swallowed frantically: ah, thank God, it's
down. He stretched out his legs and through half-closed
eyes gazed beyond the screened-in porch, the orderly gardens blurred, at once both familiar and strange, pleasur-

able yet vaguely menacing. Slowly, slowly, moving only
to reach for the mug of Ovaltine, he felt the hard sour
knot in his stomach begin to loosen and dissolve . . .
Thank heaven it was over, the waiting, the hoping, the
anticipating. He had known in his bones from the first
that Armistead would get the Jefferson Chair. But anticipating it, feeling it, knowing it intuitively, hadn't eased
the disappointment, the actual pain. Ever since that afternoon two weeks ago it had been with him constantly, turning slowly like an animal in its lair: he had been sitting in
his office in Cabell Hall, gazing from his window at the
fringe of blue mountains, when his phone had rung:
President Nelson would like to see you this afternoon,
could you come to his office sometime, say around three-
thirty?

His heart had leaped. I've got it, I've got it, by God,
I've got it! And he had had to struggle to control his
voice. Yes, he had said, very dry, very calm. Yes, tell him
I'll be glad to, three-thirty, yes.

For the remainder of the morning he had been in a fever
and he left the office early. Cancel any appointments, he
told his secretary; I have business to attend to. I will take
a long walk, he thought; *a long walk will do me good
it has been a long time since I walked up Observatory
Mountain what with meetings and appointments and con-
ferences and the thousand and one details of running a
large department   frustrating time-consuming details   pa-
perwork — problems   those two new assistant professors
activists   I'll see that those two are let go at the end of
the session   all those details   the books I've wanted to*

*write   dreamed of writing   I know now I'll never write
sleepless nights Carla muttering from her bed acting
like a slut threatening to kill herself   and the boy at Woodberry   God knows what he's up to   so many temptations
these days   why just a month ago four Woodberry boys
leaders they were   president of the student body   captain of the track team   Wayne had always wanted to be
a good runner   marijuana in their dormitory   charges
suspended   no adjudication of guilt or innocence   but
still a stigma   follow them for life and he'd been such a
good boy so loving . . .*

So he had walked alone that afternoon across what
years before had been the University golf course, now a
rolling acreage of men's residence halls, past the University
cemetery where so many of the people he had known and
two or three he had loved were resting, and then up and
around the long curving road to the Observatory, cool,
tree shaded: the redbud just beginning to flower, the dogwood blossoms still tightly furled, before long they would
open in pale green-white crosses, blood stained, and after
them from dark, almost secret places the rhododendrons
would finally burst into opulent blossoms. When he was a
small boy he had occasionally accompanied his grandfather
to Charlottesville for the monthly meetings of the Board:
the old man would leave him with friends and sometimes
after the meetings they would drive up the very road he
was now walking. *How small the University was then how
beautiful how grand the Rotunda and the Lawn and the
Ranges   how casually elegant the students in gabardines
and flannels and seersuckers not like the bearded ill-man-*

*nered unkempt pigs who since Vietnam had been flooding
into the University Trenton Detroit New York God
knows where* . . .

Halfway up the mountain he had stopped at the water-
purifying plant. It was only one-thirty; in two hours he
would be sitting in the president's office. The air was cool
but sweet, squirrels were chattering at each other through
the sun-flecked stands of pine and oak, in white foaming
fountains water sprayed from the black jets of the lagoon.
He scanned the clearing carefully, nobody was in sight,
and almost furtively he took off his shoes and loosened his
tie and half sat, half reclined at the edge of the clearing.
The hardwoods were not yet in leaf and when he looked
across and down the valley he could see the blue-green
dome of the Rotunda. Wisps of bluish smoke were rising
slowly in the thin air, rising like incense, and a feeling of
peace and contentment he had not known for years flowed
through him like pure water. Edward Nelson would rise
and shake his hand and smile knowingly: this is off the
record at this time, Web, he would say, but I wanted to
let you know . . .

He had rested there till almost three and then suddenly
his pulse had started to race, and his heart was lurching.
He swallowed two of the flat white pills, almost gagging,
and then he had turned away from the peace and the contentment and walked rapidly down the mountain, and almost before he realized it he was standing in the reception
room of the president's pavilion, chatting with his secretary
— almost too volubly. And then the president had waved
Webster into his office, more like the commons room of
an Edwardian club than an office, with comfortable leather

chairs and couches and a walnut cabinet which he knew contained champagne; they had talked casually for a minute or two and then Edward Nelson had leaned forward and in one dizzying moment, without a word being said, Webster knew that the Chair was not to be his, knew it as though the truth had been screamed at him. The floor had lurched beneath his feet. Of course, Edward, of course, he heard himself saying, his voice calm and clear and steady; I think so, I have had a departmental committee working on this since the opening of the semester, yes, I will be glad to.

So it had gone, and then he was standing outside the president's pavilion, blinking in the sunlight, and he knew that Armistead Davis was in and that he was out . . .

Webster sighed and drank the last lukewarm dregs of the Ovaltine. Armistead had always beaten him out, first with his research and then with Carla and now with the Jefferson Chair: there is not room for us both, not in the same department, not in the same university. Again he sighed, and rose heavily from the rattan chair. Tomorrow . . . today . . . would be a difficult day, there had been many difficult days, and there would be many more. He rinsed the cup and saucer and placed them in the sink; at the soft sound of footsteps he wheeled violently, his heart racing.

"Good God, what are you doing, creeping up behind me like that?"

Carla, ludicrous in her frilly knee-length baby-doll nightgown, was swaying in the pantryway, and he averted his eyes.

"You gave me a turn. I thought you had gone to sleep."

His heart was no longer fluttering and his voice was again steady. In the dimness Carla's face seemed suddenly pathetic, and he switched off the pantry light and took her arm.

"It's late, let's go to bed." His voice was not unkind, but she suddenly burst into tears, plucking the sleeve of his shirt.

"Stop that," he said. He turned his back on her and walked up the narrow stairs. He undressed slowly, placing his dinner jacket and trousers on a hanger before putting them in the closet. In the bathroom he cleaned his teeth methodically and gargled before going to bed. But sleep would not come; the air was stuffy, the bed uncomfortable. What was Carla doing, had she gone to the other bedroom as she so often did? He could not hear her, though he strained his ears in the gloom. In the morning she will probably have a hangover and there are so many things we will have to do . . . and the way she had behaved at the club . . . But I have never been able to depend on her, never. Almost from the very beginning she was a drag and a burden and a source of embarrassment, drinking too much, chattering too much, flirting too much: *Mother had been right you will regret it Webster I beg you do not marry that woman and then that disgusting business with Armistead   damn him to hell   how many years ago had it been   I should have divorced her then God knows I had provocation   but but there was the boy for his sake and besides I was coming up for promotion and that kind of divorce   what a mistake   I've always messed things up . . .*

He turned uneasily in his bed: how quiet everything was! how close the air! He felt as though he were
choking, and struggled to an upright position, straining
his ears for the sound of her breathing. Had he dozed off
and had she then, finally, returned to her bed to lie there
as she so often did, eyes half-closed, touching her nipples
beneath those idiotic nightgowns, pretending to be asleep
but quietly, furtively, fondling and stroking herself, pretending to be asleep, making love with herself?

In the dark he could not tell, so he reached cautiously
across the space between their twin beds, feeling for the
coverlet gingerly so as not to awaken her. But it was not
turned down; she must be in her own bedroom. He sighed
and rose wearily and tiptoed across the hall and peered in.
She was not there.

"Carla," he whispered, "where are you?" But the only
answer was the slight rustling of the enormous mimosa
tree in the garden and the occasional creaking of the awn-
ings from the screened-in back porch. "Damn her." He
groaned and started to return to his bed. The illuminated
dial of the clock on the bed table said two-fifteen. "How
will I get through the day with so little sleep?

"Damn her anyway," he said again, and hurried to the
head of the narrow stairs and again whispered her name,
somewhat louder than before, but the house was silent.
He went back to the bedroom, fighting to subdue a nameless choking dread: could she have wandered off somehow,
out of the house, wandering barefoot in that idiotic nightgown down the quiet Lawn, past the Colonnade Club or
along West Range? What if she were to be seen by some

drunken undergraduates, reeling home to their dormitories, how awful that would be. He shook his head savagely to clear his mind: I must dress and go look for her. He started to switch on the night-light but quickly withdrew his hand: *anyone on the Lawn might see   Wayne was right it was like living in a zoo sometimes it was hardly worth it   what in God's name has happened to her   could she had she . . . ?*

His head swam and he gripped the edge of the bed for support and very deliberately counted to ten and then to ten again, and gradually his breathing returned to normal. Had she done it, could she have done it, could she finally have done it?

He was shocked at his sudden relief — twice before she had threatened him: if you continue to treat me this way, Webster, I shall kill myself. She hoarded sleeping pills as a miser hoarded gold; he had found them in the bathroom, in her dressing table, in the junk drawer of the kitchen safe . . . Again he counted to ten before reaching for his bathrobe and rising cautiously from the bed and tiptoeing down the hall to the bathroom. He hesitated at the door, hand on the knob: *would it be better if she had? I am terrible to think that and God will punish me but I wish she were dead but not now not now.* He forced himself to open the door, cautiously, in dread; he saw her in the tub, great breasts floating loosely in the cold water, water stained cherry pink from her slashed wrists . . . or lying on the cold floor, open-mouthed, eyes glazed, an emptied phial inches away from one outstretched, stiffening hand. He shook himself and the visions vanished; he pushed the door open angrily, the bathroom was empty.

No longer tiptoeing, he hurried along the dark hall, down the narrow stairway, and into the drawing room. "Carla," he whispered, relief and disappointment mingling in his voice.

Eyes closed, she lay awkwardly on the brocaded Victorian sofa beneath the portrait of his grandfather, her nightgown in disarray above her parted thighs, her hands crossed as though in death over her slowly rising and falling bosom, almost girlish in the semidarkness. Carla, Carla, he thought, where will it ever end, and he knelt at the sofa and shook her gently. Surprisingly strong, her hand closed on his wrist as she turned to him, her eyes opening wide. "Oh Webster, Webster," she was saying thickly, "I'm sorry, sorry, sorry," and then she was sobbing, wildly, uncontrollably, her body shaking, her hair and face damp. He put his arms around her. You must be quiet, you must be quiet, someone will hear: and he placed one hand over her mouth, but her sobbing increased. He leaned over her and she half rose from the sofa, the baby-doll nightgown slipping from her, and he pushed her down, roughly, a hand on each warm shoulder. Be quiet, he whispered, raising one hand as though to slap her, but his hand stopped in midair. Slowly, slowly — he was powerless to arrest its progress — his hand descended. She reached for it and pressed it upon her breast; the full nipple was like a ripe grape beneath his fingers. She turned her open mouth upon him and he drew back, but she seized both his hands and pressed them against her, and suddenly a hot spasm of desire flamed inside him. "I'm sorry I'm sorry," she was saying, her voice muffled, and he was burning up, consumed. Her hot mouth found his, the salt stinging, the waves spreading: for God's sake, Webster, take me apart, her hot hands were on him, take me apart oh for God's sake fuck me fuck me fuck me *for God's sake Webster.*

PART 5

THE BEDCHAMBER OF THE ARCHIVIST, AFTER MIDNIGHT BUT BEFORE DAWN

When sins are dear to us we are but too prone to slide into them again, the act of repentance itself is often sweetened with the thought that it clears our account for a repetition of the same sin. Thomas Jefferson to Maria Cosway, November 19, 1786

FOGEL FREIBERG, who had fallen asleep with his head resting on Dorsey Jack Morgan's golden thighs, stirred slightly; his wild black hair formed a spectacular Rorschach pattern on the archivist's gentle belly. Watching him lazily through half-closed eyes, Dorsey smiled and ran one hand through the poet's damp and disordered curls. I should be ashamed of myself, she thought, but I'm not; I'll probably be depressed by morning but right now I feel wonderful — and she laughed aloud, a warm chuckle deep in her throat. Her eyes strayed to her right leg, grotesquely swaddled in a cumbersome walking cast on which most of the Mafia had inscribed their names and best wishes: *Good luck to Miss Morgan from her friend Raymond Green; The hell of it, I'm celibate, F. Freiberg, Esq.; Having a wonderful time wish I were there, A. D.* What a bore, she reflected, to fall into the pool that way. But even that seemed more amusing than not, and again she laughed aloud.

"What are you laughing about?" Freiberg's voice was drowsy. "Have you gone mad?" He raised his dark head and regarded her quizzically. "I think you're insane. I think we're all insane." He half closed his eyes and lowered his head, muttering. "Are you uncomfortable? I'll move if . . ."

"I'm quite comfortable . . . no, move your head just a little, though . . . ah, that's better." Miss Morgan ran her fingers through his tousled hair, and yawned. "But if in a moment or two someone nice would be good enough to get me a cigarette and fix me a drink, just a tiny one, not more than an ounce, say . . . but don't hurry, dear, wait till you're fully awake."

Again he raised his head and squinted at her. "The world has gone mad. Absolutely mad." He ran his hands through his curls reflectively. "Matter of fact I could use a short one myself. The whiskey? Where is it?"

She pointed toward the bathroom and the poet rose from the bed, shielding his genitals modestly with one cupped hand and awkwardly attempting to retrieve his trousers from the floor with the other, and again Miss Morgan suppressed a smile.

"I'd fix them myself, if it weren't for this leg."

He looked over his shoulder and grinned. "I'm glad to do it for you."

"What did you think of the party?" she asked after he had returned. "You asked me to remind you about the party."

"The party? Oh, that. I was only making conversation, I guess. I thought it was a bore. Didn't you?"

A slight frown creased the archivist's high forehead. "Oh, I don't know. It wasn't wildly entertaining but, well, it had its moments."

"Like what?" Freiberg looked at her incredulously. "Name one. Like that bitch Mrs. Eppes?" He made an angry, gagging sound. "She belongs in a zoo. You people . . ." He shrugged helplessly. "Funny she's not. Character impersonations! I thought they'd gone out with the Eisenhower administration." He leaned forward and stroked Dorsey's soft shoulder, and again waved his hands helplessly. "I may be just a New York schmuck, but obscene imitations of Martha Mitchell and Henry Kissinger!" His voice sank almost to a whisper, and he spoke more to himself than to the woman at his side. "How can you stand that sort of thing? A bore, your Mrs. Eppes is. Worse than that, she's a very bad woman, no warmth, no goodness." His voice rose angrily and he glared at the archivist. "Immoral, she is. How can you stand spending your life with buffaloes like that?"

"Really, Fogel." Dorsey Jack Morgan's eyes flashed but suddenly she began to laugh in spite of her irritation. "Let's not spoil a nice evening. You're right, of course, the impersonations *were* awful. I don't like Carla any more than you do, and I *don't* spend my life with people like that."

"Bravo!" Freiberg clapped his hands gently.

"And I wouldn't call her immoral. Pitiful, maybe, but not immoral. After all, she *is* married to Webster Eppes." The harsh lines around Freiberg's mouth and nose deepened. "Now there's a bastard's bastard for you!" He grimaced, rubbing his tongue between his teeth and lips. "I have no use for the University of Virginia, you know that, everyone around here knows it, but . . . well . . . it *has* had an honorable past." The poet's dark eyebrows formed an unbroken black frown line. "Ugh, I'm sounding like one of the schmucks from my public relations department! That Eppes!" He seized Miss Morgan's bare shoulder. "You know what he said to me tonight? After the impersonations? While his wife was in a corner rubbing her pussy against some hippie-type young guy from the History Department?"

"No." The archivist absently stroked Freiberg's writhing curls. "What did he say?"

"He said, 'People like you don't really understand the University of Virginia, Freedman.' He keeps calling me Freedman, he always does; once yesterday he even called me Epstein. He's a prince, he gets his kicks that way."

"Oh no!" Spontaneously Dorsey Jack Morgan put her arms around the poet's thin shoulders and hugged him to her. "Oh that's wicked. Do forgive us, Fogel, we're not all like that."

Freiberg drew back and intently studied her face. "Thank you, Dorsey," he said, absently patting her shoulder. "Thank you very much."

"None of us thinks very much of Webster Eppes. Don't let's talk about him anymore. Don't even think about him anymore; he isn't worth it."

"First let me tell you what he said after that."

The archivist took a sip of her drink, a very small sip.

" 'That poem of yours, Freedman. The one about the University.' It wasn't about *the* University, I said, it's about *a* university. '*The* University,' he said, without batting an eye. 'We don't like that poem around here. We don't like it even a little bit.' And then, guess what? Margaret Green, she's standing there listening and watching, the way she always does, like she's making notes or something. 'Oh but I like it very much, Professor Eppes,' she said. 'I think it's a very fine poem.'

" 'Well, *we* don't like it,' he said again, and he gave that nasty little snort of his — you know, it begins in the back of his throat, like this." Freiberg threw back his head and made a barely audible gagging sound. "And then it picks up speed, picks up speed tremendously." He repeated the action and the gagging sound increased. "And somewhere an inch or two behind his teeth, it explodes."

"You're wonderful, Fogel. Honestly, that act of yours . . ."

The poet grinned. "It's not my act; it's that schmuck's. 'You don't understand the University of Virginia, Mr. Freedman,' he says. '*Or* Thomas Jefferson either.' Then he gives that nasty little snort and stares at the Green woman and me. A real gen-u-wine dead fish stare. 'And about that poem.' "

"Really!" The archivist closed her eyes and shook her head.

"Then Green himself gets into the act. You know how sometimes he bends a little from the waist before he starts to speak? And does crazy things with his shoulders at the same time? Like this?" Freiberg revolved his shoulders as though trying to shake off a muscle spasm. "He does it unconsciously, he's prob'ly nervous or something. You know?"

"Yes." Dorsey Jack Morgan was smiling. "Yes, Fogel, I know. He's muscle-bound. From boxing."

"He's usually pretty quiet, Green. Tends to take a back seat; I think maybe he's waiting to see what way the wind's blowing."

"No, you're wrong there, Fogel. He's not waiting to see what way the wind's blowing. That's not his way. That's not Ray's way at all."

"O.K., O.K., so that's not his way. Anyhow, he steps up to us, sort of stands between us, doing those things with his shoulders. 'I think "Jefferson's Dream" is a very good poem,' he says. Then he stops and sort of catches his breath. He takes a deep breath and almost closes his eyes for a minute, the way he does, you know, his eyes are half-closed most of the time, he's nervous, prob'ly. So finally he opens his eyes and looks at Eppes. 'I think it's an excellent poem, Webster,' he says."

"Good for him! Good for Ray."

Freiberg regarded her suspiciously.

"You sort of like that guy, don't you?"

"Yes, I like him a lot. But what happened then?"

"He choked. Eppes, he almost choked. You know how pasty he is? Purple he turned, almost."

"And?"

"That's all. End of story. He just turned purple and walked away."

Dorsey made no comment but continued to stroke the poet's dark head. Inside its cast her leg seemed to be slowly expanding and she wriggled her toes experimentally.

"I do wish someone nice would mix me another small little drink."

When the poet returned, glasses in hand, she thanked him warmly.

"And what do you think of some of the rest of us?" She sipped her whiskey reflectively. "Of Armistead Davis, for example?"

"I like him." Freiberg's reply was prompt and incisive. "He's got style. He's a windbag, of course, but he's got style." The poet flattened his hair with the palms of both hands and stared at the ceiling. "What a man is like personally I couldn't care less, if I respect his work. Davis's books are first-class. Strictly first-class. So I like him. It's as simple as that." He shrugged his thin shoulders. "And he's no phony, just a very nice guy. At the National Press Club — I keep running into him, Washington, Baltimore, New York — two, three months ago, he was being interviewed about the new biography, the one Babcock had the other night; we had a long talk afterwards, before he was carried out. That's when I decided to come down here, to do a piece for the magazine. But he drinks too much; he's been drunk every time I've seen him. His books, they're the best about Jefferson there are, but the man, he's falling apart."

"Oh don't say that, Fogel. Please don't say that. You're right, of course, he does drink too much. But he never used to, it's only recently . . ." She stirred uneasily, again uncomfortably aware of her itching leg. "He's been under great strain lately. You know that, don't you?" She looked at Freiberg and smiled. "But falling apart, he's not."

The poet glared at her fiercely, but there was only amusement behind his crooked leer. "Don't mock me, Miss Morgan."

"I do it because I like you, you know that as well as I do." She stroked his dark curls and kissed the back of his neck. "But, Fogel, you know so much, you and those damned girls in your office. Just how much *do* you know? About *us?* And about those papers . . . and things?"

Freiberg stiffened and regarded Dorsey suspiciously. "You wouldn't be trying to pump me, are you?"

"Now don't you start being paranoid, dear; there's been too much of that around here already."

"O.K., O.K." His harsh voice softened. "Don't you be paranoid, either, Miss Morgan. We're — that is I'm — suspicious by nature. Something you wouldn't understand." He played with the soft hair at the base of her neck. "I know a lot more than Armistead Davis said last night. Yukkkhh, what a letdown!"

"I'm afraid you're right; ummmmm, do that some more, that feels so good."

"You or I could have given a better lecture."

"Do you think so? Ummmmm."

"Look, Dorsey, I'm a professional. No offense meant. I've spent weeks casing Jefferson, everything the girls in

the office could get their hands on. And about all of *you*."
He grinned wolfishly. "Your freaking Mafia, I could
blackmail the whole gang."

"You're impossible, Fogel. Simply *im*possible. But I
like you anyway." Suddenly serious, the archivist shook
her head reflectively and looked at Fogel Freiberg for a
long long moment. "But do be kind to Armistead in your
article. He's, he's — I know it and I guess you know it —
he's done a terrible thing, Fogel, and it's been haunting
him. That's why he's been drinking so much lately. Don't
do anything to hurt him."

"I *like* Professor Davis. I won't do anything to hurt
him."

"You are sweet, Fogel." She put her arms around the
little man's neck and kissed him. "But why were you baiting him at the Boar's Head then? About Sally Hemings
and Mrs. Cosway."

"Baiting him? So who was baiting anybody?"

"You almost broke up the party, you know; you'll be a
legend in your time, Fogel. Why did you say that? You
know very well that Maria never came to this country.
What made you say that?"

"Don't be too sure about that, Miss Morgan." A bland
smile spread across his dark face. "What would I know
about Mrs. Cosway that you don't? With Xerox, what's
secret anymore? Ask What's-his-name, the one from the
Library of Congress, with the Ben Franklin specs."

"Thorpe Taliaferro?"

"That's right, Taliaferro. If he spills cigarette ashes
in my bloody marys just once more, I'll kill him. He was

muttering to Green, Raymond Green, last night. In the gent's room at Farmington." He raised his heavy eyebrows and smiled. "After you'd left the party." He paused and looked at her suspiciously. "How come he's always whispering to Green? He was doing that on the Terrace again today . . . yesterday, I mean. There's nothing going on between those two, is there?"

The archivist laughed, a genuinely delicious laugh. "Good heavens, no. You *are* mad, Fogel. But what were they, I mean, what was Thorpe muttering about?"

Freiberg examined his fingernails. "He was using words like 'thief' and 'Dome Room' and a couple of others. Then he saw me and he stopped talking. Taliaferro, he's an ass."

"You're awful, Fogel." She shook her head slowly. "That Thorpe! Don't take anything he says too seriously."

"Don't worry, I won't. But all this is old stuff to you, and I'll tell you a little secret. Everybody in New York knows more about these papers Davis *discovered* than some of your freaking Mafia; me, I've even seen that article Davis wrote about Cosway. How does that grab you?"

"You haven't?" Miss Morgan sat upright, her breasts shaking. "How in . . . ?"

"Don't ask me how, let's not spoil a nice evening already. But do an article for me on Jefferson and Martha and the Hemings person. We pay our contributors well. Very well indeed, Miss Morgan. And Davis, he told me — at the Press Club, it was, that night — you know more about Jefferson's private life than anybody — even Snow Willoughby." He half closed his eyes and ran his fingers rapidly through his hair. "Forget Mrs. Cosway. It's Jefferson and his daughter I'm interested in."

"My leg's beginning to hurt."

The smile vanished from Freiberg's face and he rose quickly from the bed and fumbled on the floor for his crumpled clothes.

"Fogel."

He looked up irritably, but she stretched out her arms toward him.

"It really *is* getting late, and my leg *is* beginning to hurt. I'd love to do an article for you some time, really I would. I know you won't believe me, but I really don't know any more about it — the secret letters and all that — than you found out from your girls in New York. As for the article, I've heard about it, but only this weekend. If you really think Mrs. Cosway came here, you know a lot more than I do . . . but as you said, with Xerox what's secret? You are *such* a madman, Fogel; you're really insane, you know. But you're sweet, too." She added hastily, "In a very Fogelish way. I really like you. But you are insane; you know that, don't you?"

He smiled, embarrassed, pleased. "That's the nicest thing anyone's said to me in years." He fumbled for his trousers and started for the bathroom, but stopped abruptly and turned to the archivist.

"They've been talking about me, haven't they?"

"Who?"

"Damn it, Dorsey, you know who. The Mafia."

She nodded.

"What're they saying?"

"Oh, a great deal."

"They're wondering what happened to Mauve, aren't they?"

"They certainly are." Dorsey Jack Morgan stifled a yawn with the fingers of one shapely hand. "Oh, I am getting tired, Fogel; you must leave, dear. Be careful not to stumble on the stairs."

He was at her bedside, half in and half out of his trousers, his thin arms and clawlike fingers raised in vampire fashion. "What're they saying? About Mauve? And me?" He dropped his arms and sat down on the bed beside her.

"Oh, nothing much, really. Let's see." The archivist closed her eyes, pulled the coverlet to her chin, and turned on her side, addressing the wall. "Some people think she's not your wife."

"I'm flattered. That's the second nicest thing's been said about me in years. Go on."

"And Carla Eppes, she's been telling everybody she's outraged that your *waf'* hasn't been at any of the *festivities*. And she says — even though she's never even met Mauve — she saw her in *Oh! Calcutta!* Not the play, Carla never goes to the theater, but in an article about it in one of the magazines — *Cosmopolitan* or something like that, that's about her speed."

"Yukkh! Go on!"

"And I think I saw her on the 'Tonight Show.' Not so long ago."

Freiberg snorted.

"And Margaret Green . . . you know she's written a couple of whodunits."

"Yeah, everybody keeps reminding me. But she's O.K.,

except when she's making like Mrs. North or Miss Marple."

"Making like . . . ?"

"The bellboy told me she was asking him questions. Like had he seen Mrs. Freiberg or what had happened to the dog. That sort of thing. But she's O.K." Freiberg placed his arm between the coverlet and Miss Morgan's warm back, and whispered through the soft ashen hair. "What's she doing that for?"

"I heard that she thinks you've murdered Mauve."

"Mad," he muttered. "Mad . . . Why?"

"Why what? Oh Fogel, I'm getting so tired . . . And stop it, that tickles."

"Why does she think I murdered Mauve?"

"I honestly don't know, Fogel dear, maybe it's because she writes whodunits. Or maybe she doesn't *really* think so, she's just having some fun. I expect that's it. Why don't you ask her?"

"I will, by God, tomorrow."

"Good, dear, I think that's very sensible of you." Dorsey snuggled deeper into her bedclothes, but Freiberg shook her gently until she turned and looked at him through half-closed eyes. "Ummmmhhh?" she murmured, more as a statement than a question.

"And what do *you* think?" The poet's voice was softly insinuating.

"Think? About what, dear Fogel?"

"Don't give me that dear Fogel routine. About Mauve. What do you think about Mauve? You're not interested in knowing where she is?"

"Not really, dear. I haven't really been thinking about Mauve at all."

"Or about our *cockerel* spaniel? You're not interested in him?"

She smiled and again turned toward the wall and closed her eyes.

Freiberg shook himself, as much in amusement as irritation. "And you call *me* incredible!" He leaned over and brushed his lips against the nape of her neck. "What would you say if I told you I *had* killed her?"

"I wouldn't believe you." Miss Morgan burrowed still more deeply into the lavender-scented blankets. "Do turn off the hall light before you go out, dear. And be careful going down the stairs."

"Incredible!" Shaking his head in disbelief Freiberg reached for the light switch, but withdrew his hand and took a few uncertain steps toward the bedroom. "What would you say if I told you she just took the goddamned dog and left? To visit Jackie and Aristide or whatever his name is. On Scorpio already."

"Oh, Fogel." The archivist's voice was barely audible. "Don't be silly."

Freiberg ran his fingers desperately through his hair. "That first night. When you were jumping into the swimming pool." He half closed his eyes, speaking more to himself than to the quiet figure in the bed. "What would you say if I told you she left then? What would you say if I told you her agent called her about a screen test? What — ?"

"I'd believe that, Fogel." Miss Morgan stifled a yawn. "That's exactly what the receptionist at the desk told me.

This afternoon. After we came back from . . . from Michie Tavern. Good night, Fogel dear."

The poet closed his eyes and shook his head slowly. "Mad," he muttered, and turned and walked unsteadily back to the door and switched off the light. "You're all mad."

At the sound of the closing door Dorsey Jack Morgan smiled in the darkness. It is a good night for sleeping, I can sleep late. But I must get in touch with Armistead, first thing. Ummmm. That Fogel!

PART 6

A FRAGMENT FROM THE JOURNAL OF HELEN DAVIS, 2:30 A.M.

This world abounds indeed with misery. to lighten its burthen we must divide it with another. Thomas Jefferson to Maria Cosway, October 12, 1786

I AM WAITING here in our room. It is two-thirty in the morning. I am waiting for Armistead. I do not know where he is, he and Rodney disappeared after a reception given for them at the Colonnade Club. I have finally decided to kill Armistead, he no longer deserves to live, he is

a sinner and I am glad I have decided to kill him . . . I
have thought about this a long time oh so many hours so
many   I should have done it before but I was afraid no not
afraid I wondered how and then I found out how and oh
such a blessed relief I feel clean purged washed . . .

CHAPTER 12

THE BANQUET

All my wishes end where I hope my days will end, at Monticello. Thomas Jefferson to George Gilmer, August 11, 1787

CARLA EPPES pushes aside her partially emptied dish of crème brûlée and leans forward, her bosom spectacular above the décolletage of her dinner dress, a gown the color of the walls and the Wedgwood medallions in the fireplace mantel of the dining room at Monticello. Candles everywhere: at the table of honor the faces of the Mafia are softened in their gentle light. Carla gazes smugly at her reflection in the tall French window behind the table. Behind and beyond the window a massive magnolia tree blooms in the velvet of the April night. She shifts her silk-encased buttocks in the black leather seat of a Hepplewhite chair, and casts a disapproving glance at the vacant place at her elbow from which Arthur, the head steward, has some time ago discreetly removed the placecard bearing the name of Thorpe Taliaferro. Again Carla leans forward, turning her bright eyes on the gravely handsome man at the head of the table. Her lips form the words *disgustin', Edward, absolutely disgustin',* but the president of the University either does not hear or chooses to ignore her remark.

Poor Thorpe. Margaret Green smiles across the table at Dorsey Jack Morgan, who almost imperceptibly lifts one shoulder and inclines her shining head toward Carla be-

fore knowingly acknowledging Margaret's glance. Poor
Thorpe, he's had it for good this time . . .

. . .

How beautiful it had been, driving up that dark road
with Raymond just two hours ago. *Up the silent twisting
road to Mr. Jefferson's mountaintop   through the black
trees a quick glimpse of the house glowing like some
enchanted place   inside the great Entrance Hall champagne and conversation and from the unseen parlor beyond the dining room the strains of an early Mozart string
quartet Armistead Davis silver-headed in the candlelight Dorsey Jack Morgan statuesque in spite of the
walking cast with its scrawled assortment of signatures
and comments   Fogel Freiberg spectacular in a cranberry-
colored frilled dress shirt spilling over the broad lapels
of his lemon dinner jacket like a wave at high tide   all
the Mafia present and accounted for except Helen Davis where could she be   she and Raymond exhilarated
slightly high   drawn to the portrait of Martha Jefferson Randolph Mister Jefferson's own dear Patsy   that
face more mysterious than ever in the candlelight   more
poignant those sad sad eyes slightly mocking too
thoughts past echoes dark secrets long-dead passions seventeen or eighteen she was when she and
Thomas Mann Randolph and fresh from five years in
Paris I am reluctant minister plenipotentiary how
could such a marriage succeed   Electra Oedipus what I
hold most is your satisfaction   indeed I should be miserable without it eleven children the Colonel Martha
Maria Cosway Peter Carr Sally Hemings hidden stairs*

*and underground passages   silently silently   what did he
really look like   rawboned   swarthy as an Indian   peeled
the skin from Bankhead's forehead   insensible   leave me
to my fields and my poetry   there should be a portrait
of him here   here by his Martha   Jefferson had loved
him   I now see by our fireside   pride and love   please
return   be a member of the family   I am a goose who
cannot feel at ease among swans   what I hold most precious   I am the most unquiet impatient being   is your
satisfaction   my life is a torment   I could flee to the grave
would not set foot   hated his own son   would not even
sit at deathbed   I am but   Martha collapsed   excessive
languor and sadness . . .*

"That's a stupid thing to say, Thorpe. A very stupid
thing."

Armistead Davis's voice, surprisingly harsh. Hair silken-
soft, he stared at Thorpe Taliferro, Craig Babcock beside them pausing uncertainly, his raised half-filled glass
of champagne frozen in the act of proposing a toast. They
had hastened from the portrait; Margaret slipped her
hand into the cradle of Armistead's arm, and beneath her
fingers tensed muscles relaxed ever so slightly.

"How . . . how lovely you look, Margaret." Turned
his back on the librarian, bowed, swaying ever so slightly:
tanned forehead beaded with tiny droplets, cigarette
ashes on lapels of dinner jacket. Thorpe, too, groping in
their direction, without his glasses naked, vulnerable.

"Oh, uh, hello, Margaret." Voice thick, dark bruise on
the knuckles of one hand, knees of his trousers dirt-stained.
"Arm'stead and I . . ." Shook his head. "I broke my
glasses." Fumbled in his pocket, retrieved the ruins, ex-

tended them in cupped hands toward her. "I can't see a thing."

"Ray, help him."

Staggered against them, clutching wildly at her shoulders: a moment of blank fright, he will tumble me to the floor with him, but Raymond caught him beneath the arms and she righted herself quickly: Mrs. Pennyfeather had appeared as though on a magic carpet and they had helped him from the hall, feet dragging, mumbling incoherently.

A hush, amused, embarrassed, tragicomic: and the voice of Carla Eppes.

"Disgustin'. Simply disgustin'."

. . .

Now the waiters have removed the dessert dishes: at the table of honor only Mr. Jefferson's epergne of Waterford glass sparkles coldly like the stars above the skylight in the center of the high ceiling, scattering splinters of light on the satiny surface of the Chippendale table which, Mrs. Pennyfeather had informed Margaret the day before, had been a gift from Jefferson's Williamsburg friend and law teacher, the celebrated jurist George Wythe. There will be another toast, Margaret reflects as the waiters enter with trays of fresh wineglasses: how many have we had already? These Virginians! what guzzlers! One to the Queen of England before the first course, *oeufs farcis* and *filets anchois cresson* according to the blue leather-bound souvenirs at each guest's service plate; the second like the first in Amontillado to the President of the United States; and then one in Château Lafitte 1953 to the memory of Mr. Jefferson and then . . . I wonder what this will be . . .

Arthur ceremoniously removes a decanter from the dumbwaiter beside the fireplace. "It's not used anymore," Craig is saying. "Jefferson designed it, of course. In his day it was connected with the wine cellar" — he points beneath them — "it's near the kitchen, you know. The wine cellar's empty now, of course, and so's the kitchen . . . everything's catered from Charlottesville." He waves his great arms apologetically. "But I still like to serve the Madeira from the dumbwaiter. Ah, thank you, Arthur."

The wine is passed, the curator glances up and down the table; he takes a deep breath and heaves his vast bulk from the chair. Self-consciously he straightens the cuffs of his shirt. From the parlor the last sounds of a Boccherini quartet fade away, accompanied by the scraping of chairs and shuffling of feet from the tearoom adjoining the dining room, where auxiliary tables have been set up for the officers of the Jefferson Foundation and other guests.

"As a general rule we don't have any speeches at this dinner, but tonight" — Craig smiles at Armistead Davis who, seated at his right, is inhaling the fragrance of mingled mahogany, grape, and smoke from the dark wine in his glass — "tonight is different. Tonight is something special. As you all know, as you heard at Cabell Hall last night and as I expect you read in the paper today, we have with us tonight the newly designated recipient of the Thomas Jefferson Chair of History at the University of Virginia." He pauses at the mild flurry of applause, holds up one huge hand. "And he's going to say a few things to-

night." Flushing, Craig smiles again at Armistead and
lifts his glass as everyone gets to his feet. "Ladies and gentlemen, I give you the first Jefferson scholar in the world
today . . . *and* the first holder of the Jefferson Chair . . .
a man who needs no introduction here. To Armistead
Davis."

"I appreciate that," Armistead says after the toast has
been drunk and the hand-clapping and general murmur-
ing have subsided. His voice is husky, so low that the people in the tearoom have to strain their ears as he puts
down his glass and fumbles in his pocket. "I appreciate
that very much. More than I can say." He coughs, withdraws a long black cigarette holder from his pocket, and
plays with it absently, passing it from one hand to the
other. "I'm going to talk briefly about some matters I'd
originally planned to discuss last night. But for various
reasons . . ." He hesitates, and smiles, the old infectious
Davis smile. "For various reasons — such as the thumb-
screw, the rack, and the iron maiden, to name only three
— I changed my mind. For various reasons, and at the re-
quest of my old and very good friend." He looks across
the table at John Rodney, ruddy, gnomelike, and very
attentive.

"Hear, hear." Rodney's voice is barely audible in the
ripple of subdued laughter.

"So tonight I want to talk about some of the things I
didn't say last night." Armistead runs the fingers of one
hand through his silver hair; he is beginning to sweat pro-
fusely. "Some of these matters are not the most pleasant
in the world." At the sudden gravity of his tone the laughter dies away before ever really being born.

"As a lifetime admirer of Mr. Jefferson . . ." Again he pauses as though fumbling for the exact word. The damned showboat, Webster Eppes is thinking. How old, how tired he looks, it seems to Dorsey, who feels a sudden compassion mingled with an exhilarating sense of liberation; and she steals a look at the small dark figure of Fogel Freiberg, who is intently studying Armistead and twirling his empty glass between a gnarled thumb and forefinger. "I am distressed," Armistead resumes, clearing his throat with a palpable effort, "even appalled, by some . . . some recent discoveries."

Craig Babcock shakes his huge head and automatically reaches for his wineglass. A slow flush spreads upward from the collar of his dress shirt and he uneasily slips the tip of his index finger between his neck and collar.

"But at the same time, as a historian, as a seeker for the truth, I am fascinated by them. Distressed and fascinated." At the unsteadiness of his voice Margaret finds herself wondering: is this an act? Armistead reaches for his water tumbler, it is empty; he unobtrusively beckons the always attentive Arthur. "But before I discuss these matters, I have a few preliminary comments." He turns to Craig Babcock. "And, later, I will have an explanation. I am aware, and I regret and deplore this enormously, that recently there has been considerable speculation concerning these discoveries. Speculation concerning whether, indeed, they actually exist . . . and, if so, how I came upon them."

He returns his cigarette holder to his pocket and sips the remainder of his Madeira. Scanning the table, he catches by turn the eyes of each guest. Craig again shakes his head, Webster Eppes looks the other way, Dorsey Jack Morgan smiles warmly as does Margaret, Freiberg makes the peace gesture, his hands an inch or two above the table-top, John Rodney lifts his eyebrows while his mouth forms a small puckered O, Carla blushes and like her husband looks the other way, Raymond shuffles his feet and reaches in his pocket for his dark glasses, President Nelson studies the last drops of his Madeira. There is a hum of small sighs and discreet *ohhh*s and *mmmm*s. Arthur enters with a pitcher and a water-filled glass on a silver tray which he places before Armistead, who drinks thirstily.

"Let me say, ladies and gentlemen, they *do* exist. And they *are* authentic." His voice is stern, so stern that to Margaret it seems as though the pleasure of the occasion has faded away like the music of the string quartet. "And they are important." He glances quickly at Dorsey Jack Morgan, who again smiles at him, and his eyes linger on the dark face of Fogel Freiberg, who twirls his wineglass speculatively; John Rodney makes as though to reach out to touch Armistead but withdraws his hand. The chill moment is broken by the clearing of someone's throat from the tearoom.

"These discoveries have to do with problems which have interested me, have interested all Jeffersonians for a long time." He reaches for his cigarette holder, inserts and lights a fresh cigarette, inhales deeply. Are her eyes deceiving her, Margaret wonders, or is he swaying ever so slightly? "Not major problems, perhaps, in the sense of having profound . . . historic import, but of great importance to our understanding . . . our understanding of the kind of man, the kind of human being, Mr. Jefferson was. For these are all highly . . . highly *personal* discoveries, ladies and gentlemen, long-lost family letters, plantation records of Mr. Jefferson's overseers, personal memorabilia."

Armistead's voice has sunk almost to a whisper; he reaches for the water glass which Craig Babcock has been replenishing, meanwhile brandishing his cigarette holder with the other hand. "The problem is, first of all, concerned with Mr. Jefferson's relations, if I may use the term, with his daughter. With Martha Jefferson Randolph." He takes a deep breath. "And with her husband, Colonel Thomas Mann Randolph."

He removes a white handkerchief from the sleeve of his dinner jacket and wipes his mouth and forehead; the tension in the room is increasing, and Margaret is uncomfortably aware of the sweat collecting in the hollows of her armpits and thighs. "And, though I know this is offensive to some of you, with the woman Sally Hemings, Monticello Sally. As I have said, some of these are not pleasant things." He studies the tip of his cigarette before again inhaling deeply; the accumulated ash drops unheeded upon the front of his dinner jacket. "As most of you know, Thomas Mann Randolph was, shall we say" — he closes his eyes and shakes his head quickly before resuming, his voice momentarily stronger, the color returning to his handsome face — "eccentric, strong-willed, of a passionate, indeed, highly unstable nature. You know, too, that Martha, Mrs. Randolph, was inor —— inordi —— "

Armistead Davis sways forward and reaches for the table. Alarmed, Craig starts to rise from his chair.

"I'm sorry, I'm sorry." The biographer raises one hand

apologetically. "I'm very tired." A spasm contorts his features; he doubles over, fingers outstretched, the black cigarette holder clatters to the table; he clutches both shoulders with his hands and despite Craig Babcock's protective lunge and amidst the cries of the guests crashes to the table like a falling tree.

CHAPTER 13

A CATASTROPHE IN
THE HOUSE

*A single event wiped away all my plans
and left a blank which I had not the
spirits to fill up.* Thomas Jefferson to
the Marquis de Chastellux, November
26, 1782

B ENEATH THEM the University Grounds had faded away in a blur of green and red and white. Raymond patted Margaret's hand before removing his hand from hers, and they pushed their seats into reclining positions.

"It seems a long time since we came in there." She gestured below and behind them.

"A very long time," he said, and reached for a cigarette.

He had been smoking constantly since Armistead Davis had crossed his arms across his chest, tightly as though to hug away the sudden devastating pain, gripped a shoulder with each hand, and fallen face down upon the table at Monticello. Margaret would never forget the look that had flashed across that suddenly ashen face, a look not of pain or consternation or alarm but rather of apology, as though he were somehow committing an antisocial or ungentlemanly act, as though he were about to say, Look, dears, I'm terribly sorry about all this, this is such a bore, do forgive me, will you . . . ?

An athlete to the end, he had made a last-second effort to break the fall, hands with outstretched fingers warding off the unseen opponent, before he had crashed into the pitcher of water. The whole long gleaming table seemed to reverberate with the impact . . . she would hear that impact again and again, Margaret knew, could hear it, see it now. A blur of horror: the thud of that handsome head, the broken glass, the overturned pitcher. Armistead had tried once to rise, had raised his head and lifted one hand as though to brush away the trail of blue smoke rising from his still-burning cigarette, and then he had collapsed, had started to slide to the floor slowly, so terribly slowly, but Craig Babcock had caught him beneath the arms and gently, like a mother with a sick child, cradled him in his massive arms and eased him onto the taupe carpet. He had turned to Raymond: For God's sake, call the medical center, quick!

Gasping, bubbling sounds had issued from Armistead's slack mouth. Craig had loosened his black tie and torn open the collar of his dress shirt, the old-fashioned gold collar button twinkling to the floor. Get some brandy, he kept saying, and please, you all, keep back; Meg, will you get them out of here, please?

Mrs. Pennyfeather had returned with the brandy, followed by Arthur, a look of such anguish and concern on his black face that tears stung Margaret's eyes. Please, you all, Craig said again, and the guests had left the room, slowly, almost somnambulistically; averting their eyes from the figure on the carpet, as though they were unwilling voyeurs, forced witnesses to something somehow degrading, shameful, ignominious. Stay with me, Rod, and you too, Meg, Craig had said, and very gently they had raised Armistead's head and held the brandy to his lips and tried to force down a few drops, but most of the pale liquid had dribbled from the corners of his twisted mouth.

God, why don't they get here? Craig had unbuttoned

Armistead's dress shirt and ripped apart his T-shirt. He placed his ear against the still-strong and muscular chest which was rising and falling spasmodically, and then he had looked up at Margaret and the small, somehow shrunken figure of John Rodney, and had shaken his head gravely. Then Raymond was kneeling beside them: They're sending an emergency unit from the medical center, he had said, and he squeezed Margaret's hand and turned away from Armistead's ashen face . . .

Sirens soon wailed up the dark road, attendants in white uniforms carried a folded wheeled cot and an oxygen tank into the dining room, and she and Raymond had tiptoed away. In the Entrance Hall someone, Mrs. Pennyfeather or Arthur probably, had turned on the electric lights, but the still-burning candles cast pale and grotesque silhouettes on the greenish walls. A few guests remained, in silent groups or alone; beside the Sully portrait, the first violinist from the string quartet awkwardly cradled his instrument in his lap. No one spoke as Raymond and Margaret entered but everyone turned toward them expectantly, worry and concern on their drawn faces as though to ask: how is he, for God's sake tell us he's all right; and all Raymond did was shake his head and mutter: I don't know, I don't know anything. He had put on his dark glasses; he was struggling to control his voice. I don't know, he repeated almost angrily, but the doctor is there, they're doing everything they can. He had tightened his grip on Margaret's arm and together they left the hall and stood on the porch behind the tall white columns. Raymond was crying silently, it was the first time Margaret had ever seen him cry, and he had withdrawn his hand and walked alone down the broad brick walkway, tree-lined and facing the distant mountains.

Then the other guests were walking past her to their cars. Mrs. Pennyfeather had told them that Craig thought they should leave, no they did not know how *he* was; but Craig had instructed Mrs. Pennyfeather to suggest that they all leave, there was nothing to be gained by their waiting, he would get in touch with all of them as soon as possible. And Raymond had returned from the white gates — they were the only ones left in the cool night — and without speaking they had started down the wooden steps to the parking lot when they heard Craig calling: Ray, wait. He was standing in the L of the South Pavilion and the Promenade to the house, where the day before Margaret had waited for Raymond and speculated on the mysteries that Colonel Randolph's Study might conceal. They met Craig halfway up the walkway and they *knew* from the set of his broad shoulders. He is dead, was all Craig said, Armistead is dead. He had insisted, in spite of their protestations, that they return to the Boar's Head: there is nothing you can do, I will call you if I need you, no, honestly, I think you should go. They had walked without speaking to their car and it was not until they were halfway down the mountain, past the graveyard, the great obelisk pale in the darkness, and could see the lights of Charlottesville and the University across the Rivanna River, that Margaret had started forward in her seat, her hand flying to her throat.

"Helen! Good heavens, Ray, has anyone told Helen?"

CHAPTER 14

OFF WE GO, INTO THE
WILD BLUE

*Take care of me when dead, and be
assured that I shall leave with you my
last affections.* Thomas Jefferson to
James Madison, February 17, 1826

THEY HAD RETURNED to the Boar's Head almost without speaking, and Raymond had stayed a long time under the shower. It was past midnight when they finally lay down on the great bed, Raymond smoking and staring up at the hand-hewn ceiling beams. Should we call Helen, Margaret had asked as they had driven slowly through the silent streets of Charlottesville, but after some hesitation he had shaken his head. We don't know her that well, it would be . . . it would be presumptuous. I think we should call, she had said again; no, he maintained, turning his eyes from the ceiling, Craig will see to it, and just then the phone on the bed table had buzzed.

"What is it, Craig, what's . . . Hold on, just a minute, will you?" Raymond's voice was unsteady, the color was draining from his face, and the telephone almost slipped from his fingers.

"Incredible. For God's sake, no. *Not* a heart attack? I don't believe it. But . . ."

"In the cigarette holder? Poison? Are you sure? But who?"

"Helen? Christ Almighty! She left a confession?"

"Oh no. Incredible."

"Tomorrow? An inquest?"

"Yes. Yes, of course I'll be there. I can come now if
you want me to. I can — "

"Are you sure? Are you sure you don't want me to come
out now?"

"Tomorrow then. Good God in Heaven!"

He had replaced the receiver, and sat down beside her
on the bed, his head in his hands.

"I guess you could tell what's happened from that," he
said, and switched off the light. "When Craig called her
at the hotel she was already dead. The coroner and the
police were already there. Je*sus* Christ. She'd spelled it
all out in a confession note, too. It was, I can't remember
exactly, what he said sounded something like methyphos-
. . . methyl- . . . something like that, but . . . Let's
not talk about it now."

.   .   .

"I still don't believe it." Margaret's voice was positive;
they had lingered over breakfast in their room, and in
spite of the events of the preceding night she felt surprisingly — almost ashamedly — good. "Helen had the provocation, Lord knows, and I guess she'd wished for it,
dreamed about it, for a long time. She'd certainly planned
is carefully, the note and her diary prove that. But, damn
it, Ray, can't you see? She's too much of a lady. People
like that don't murder. Oh of course they *have,* but very
rarely. They can plan it, get the means — there're any
number of lethal inhalants; they can kill you in five minutes or almost instantly, depending on how much is inhaled, or death could occur, say up to twenty-four hours.
There're nerve gases, terrible things, I've read a lot about

them; Tabun and Soman are the common names. But not Helen. People like Helen, they don't, I tell you, they don't murder. Wait till the — the autopsy."

. . .

Now they were flying over the same farmland where less than a week ago Raymond had seen the single farmer on his tractor working the field of freshly turned reddish earth, but today the land was invisible, they were flying heavily through swirling clouds, and Raymond's forehead was furrowed and slightly damp.

"I'm glad we took that Dramamine before we left Charlottesville. We'll probably be stacked up over Washington. God Almighty." Uneasily he tightened his seat belt — the warning signal had flashed on a few moments before — and stared morosely into the gray void outside their window. "It'll be good to get home, Meg, it's been a long time."

She carefully turned down the page corner, and laid her book on her lap. "It *will* be good. Oh, Ray, I'm so sorry; it was awful the way things turned out. But there's some consolation that Helen didn't actually do it, that it *was* a heart attack after all."

Gently Raymond rubbed the bridge of his nose. "Your first, I mean your second, trip to Virginia." Almost without thinking he glanced forward, half-expecting to see Fogel Freiberg, hair writhing, irritably examining the contents of the magazine rack. "It wasn't quite what I'd, uh, anticipated . . ."

. . .

They had sat up late the night after the private memorial services for Armistead and Helen Davis. After leaving Margaret at the Boar's Head they had driven slowly
out to Monticello and the quiet of Craig Babcock's clut-
tered study. "Why did he do it?" Raymond had asked after his third bourbon. "Why in God's name did he do it?"

"Who knows, Raymond? Why does *any*body do *any*thing
wrong?" John Rodney had made his habitual Latin shrug
of bewilderment. "That doctor down in Mathews Court-
house some time ago; you remember him, Craig. A much-
loved, highly respected man. And one day, after he'd
treated his last patient, he dismembered his nurse. Kept
some of the remains in the icebox for a week before he was
apprehended." Thoughtfully he rubbed his temples as
though to comfort a dull persistent ache. "Public officials
— I knew a lot of them in France and Italy — honorable
men for years and then suddenly they start cheating the
government, or defect to the East, or God knows what-all.
And here at home, cabinet members, people you respect,
even the President, telling lies, committing perjury on
national television . . ." He glanced at Craig Babcock,
half-slumped behind his desk. "I think I'll have some
more vermouth, Craig . . . Beckett and Ionesco are right.
It's an absurd world."

"I still can't see why he did it." Raymond sipped his
whiskey absently. "He'd have had first rights on most of
the new stuff anyhow, wouldn't he? Won't everything go
through your hands first, Craig? Before it winds up at
Princeton or Washington or here at the University?"

The curator paused in the act of refilling John Rodney's

glass. "I should imagine so. What do you think, Rod? Where are they now? Did Armistead say? Sorry, here's your vermouth."

"He said they were back in Cambridge." John Rodney stretched painfully, passing his glass beneath his nose, inhaling the aroma with obvious pleasure. "Lord, I'm tired, I need to get back to the farm." He waved one hand as if in apology. "We sat up till around three after that party at the Colonnade Club. He was really wound up; he was on one of those talking jags, you all know how he could get. Insisted that I come back to the hotel with him, he wanted to drink and talk all night. He felt bad about the whole thing, very bad, Craig." Gratefully the novelist sipped his drink. "About how he got the papers — they were up there in the Sky Room — everybody knows that now. But *why* he didn't tell you . . . I don't think he knew himself. But it was killing . . ." John Rodney's sunburned face darkened and he bit his lips and shook his head angrily. "I mean he was hurting, deep inside he was hurting, but he was determined to keep them from anybody else — from Julian Boyd and the Princeton people or the Library of Congress or that outfit on the West Coast. Said they were in a safe-deposit box and they'd stay there until — "

"That's not like Armistead. He'd always been so, uh, generous with everybody. Like with Dorsey; he let her have all those Cosway letters for her book, and God knows what he's given Craig and me."

"That was quite different, Ray." Again John Rodney shrugged helplessly. "And that was some time ago, too.

He *wanted* those new things for himself and no one else, they were that important to him. I couldn't understand it either."

The curator leaned forward in his chair. "Did he say what they were?"

"Not specifically. Except for Mrs. Cosway. He did say there was evidence — not proof, mind you — but evidence that maybe, only *maybe*, she *had* come to America for a while. But not here, not to Monticello."

"Well, I'm damned." Craig Babcock shook his head in amazement. "That joker Freiberg. I wonder how he found out about *that?*"

John Rodney again inhaled the bouquet from his glass and took a slow, thoughtful sip of the pale liquid. "Armistead didn't say — but he mentioned an article about it — a fairly general one, I gathered — he'd done for one of the New York magazines."

"That little son of a bitch! It was probably one of those damned girls in his office . . . But I still don't believe it, Rod. About Mrs. Cosway being here, I mean. What about the rest?" Craig grimaced. "About Sally Hemings?"

"Again, he wasn't specific. But he said there was enough to lay that old ghost." Rodney smiled as the curator, breathing a great sigh of relief, sank back in his chair. "Nothing to suggest there was really anything between Jefferson and her. I expect it was one of the nephews. But there was a drawing, or maybe it was a water color — that'd be a real discovery, wouldn't it? — of Sally, apparently by that brother of hers, the one who made the chairs. *And* a letter. He was terribly excited about a letter, but he wouldn't go into any detail."

"God Almighty! And Martha? And Thomas Mann Randolph?" Craig Babcock's voice was tense.

John Rodney shook his head. "I don't really know. He simply wouldn't talk about that. It was getting late, and he'd had a lot too much to drink; maybe he was just running out of gas. But he said he really had something *big* there. That was what he *really* wanted to keep from everyone else. I just don't know, Craig."

· · ·

The plane gave a sudden dipping lurch and Raymond drew in his breath sharply: God damn these Piedmont planes! With some difficulty he withdrew a handkerchief from his hip pocket and wiped his forehead, shaking his head at Margaret's you-don't-feel-sick-do-you; you're-not-going-to-be-sick-are-you? He smiled somewhat wanly and fumbled for his tote bag beneath the seat; after a moment or two of searching he took out a miniature bottle of bourbon.

"Surely you're not going to drink that straight, Ray?" She shook her head as he offered her the bottle. "Yes, I see that you are. Don't worry, darling, we'll be in Washington in a very few minutes."

He returned the emptied bottle to his tote bag, exhaled slowly, and refastened his seat belt, as she smiled, reopened her book, and began to read.

"Mescal," said the Consul.
The main barroom of the Farolito was deserted. From a mirror behind the bar, that also reflected the door open to the square, his face silently glared at him, with stern, familiar foreboding.

Yet the place was not silent. It was filled by that ticking: the ticking of his watch, his heart, his conscience, a clock somewhere. There was a remote sound, too, from far below, of rushing water, of subterranean collapse; and moreover he could still hear them, the bitter wounding accusations he had flung at his own misery . . .

Poor Armistead, she thought, and turned down the page. *So much talent so much knowledge so much vitality all gone wasted the Chair who would get the Chair now surely not Webster Eppes it will have to be Webster Raymond had said after all it was between him and Armistead in the beginning oh no not Webster not that cold dry man who else she had asked what about Dumas Malone ever since we arrived people have been talking about Dumas Malone he is beyond the age Ray had said it's like any other academic appointment mandatory retirement at seventy or he would have been the recipient from the beginning it would be a shame for someone like Webster to get the chair Dorsey Jack Morgan had told her while Raymond was still upstairs they were waiting in the lobby of the Boar's Head for Craig to take them to the airport now don't breathe a word of this Margaret but there is a possibility that Ray might be nominated good heavens you can't mean that he's too young isn't he that's true she had said but I think President Nelson isn't too keen on Web and after all he was made president of the University when he was in his early forties no older than Ray is now besides he knows Ray's work and knows how much Armistead thought of the new book but don't breathe a word and then Ray had stepped out of the elevator we'll keep you informed I hope he gets it . . .*

. . .

Again the plane lurched, and Raymond put on his dark glasses. "Never again," he muttered, more to himself than to Margaret. "You'll never get me to set foot in a plane again. But, Meg, if we get home alive, the next time we go to see your folks, I'm going to buy that merry-go-round horse." He closed his eyes and reached for Margaret's hand, shifting uneasily in his seat and opening one eye long enough to study the thumb he had just nicked when he had refastened his seat belt. "Love you, Meg," he whispered, his voice barely audible above the straining motors, and again he closed his eyes and started counting, counting and waiting uneasily for the first signs that they were approaching the Washington airport.